CW00842933

Final Justice

M. A. COMLEY

ISBN-13: 978-1505646375

ISBN-10: 1505646375

OTHER BOOKS BY
NEW YORK TIMES BEST SELLING AUTHOR
M. A. COMLEY

Cruel Justice

Impeding Justice

Final Justice

Foul Justice

Guaranteed Justice

Ultimate Justice

Virtual Justice

Hostile Justice

Tortured Justice

Rough Justice (coming Jan 2015)

Blind Justice (A Justice novella)

Evil In Disguise (Based on true events)

Forever Watching You (#1 D I Miranda Carr Thrillers)

Torn Apart (Hero Series #1)

End Result (Hero Series #2)

Sole Intention (Intention Series #1)

Grave Intention (Intention Series #2)

It's A Dog's Life (A Lorne Simpkins short story)

ACKNOWLEDGMENTS

As always love and best wishes to my wonderful Mum for the role she plays in my career. Special thanks to my superb editor Stefanie, and my wonderful cover artist Karri. Thanks also to Joseph my amazing proof reader.

Licence Notes.

Chapter One

A Chateau in Normandy
September 2009

Baldwin smiled smugly as he surveyed his lavish surroundings, self-congratulation exuding from every pore. That night would be all about him, his ability to manipulate others, as months of meticulous planning came to fruition.

A few the scantily clad girls, all of Eastern-European extraction, giggled in the corner. He scowled at them, realising they'd been helping themselves to the potent punch, intended for his esteemed guests.

With the final tune-up complete, the band members drifted off to get changed. Meanwhile, the experienced agency staff tinkered, adding the finishing touches to the thirty-foot table, laden with some of the world's finest food, specially imported for the night's soirée.

Baldwin's gaze drifted out over the large terrace, and he took in the incredible view, the view that had sold him on the chateau. Thirty acres of manicured lawns, bordered by hedges shaped like animals—luxurious surroundings more suited to royalty than a lad brought up—or, rather, dragged up—in the boarded-up slums of Salford, Manchester. A lad with a rap sheet longer than the Seine.

Most of his men were already standing in position, their weapons safely concealed beneath their smart tuxedos. They would be joined by the others once the limos arrived.

Baldwin glanced at his watch for the tenth time in as many minutes, his irritation bubbling just below the surface. The guests should have arrived at seven, a full ten minutes before; where the bloody hell were they? He marched over to the window and craned his neck to look up the long tree-lined drive.

Nothing, not a limo in sight—nothing but the grey gravel, glistening in the evening sun. It didn't bode well, not in his book, anyway. His blood pumped harder, faster, and he felt the familiar vein jut out on his temple, just as it always did when something didn't go according to plan. *His* plan.

"Well?" he asked, when Julio, his second in command, joined him at the window.

"Nothing as yet, boss. Everything's ready, though."

"That much I can see, you bloody moron. Now go and see what the fucking hold-up is. I want this evening to go smoothly. You understand, Julio: no cock-ups."

"Yes, boss. I'll get onto it straight away."

"Never mind. I'll see for myself. I know how those guys can twist you round their fingers." Baldwin stormed into the communications room next door. The room was littered with pizza boxes, and a bottle of scotch sat on the desk in front of his men. The three men, all built like bouncers, leapt to their feet.

"Look at the bloody mess in here! Did I say you could drink on duty? This is supposed to be serious business tonight. I'm warning you: fuck this up, and you'll pay for it—with your *lives*. You got that? Now, what's the bloody hold-up?" He glared. The men nodded like toy dogs in the back of a car.

Glaring, Baldwin stepped forward. He stopped in front of the youngest of the three men, their noses a few inches apart. "I said, 'Have you got that?' Benji?"

The man gulped, his eyes bulging with fear. He nodded again. "Yes, boss. I got it."

"This is your final warning, Benji. Screw this up, and…" Baldwin left the sentence unfinished on purpose.

The new recruit backed away, and Baldwin let him go—for the time being. He'd had his eye on Benji for a while. The man's attitude stank. It hadn't escaped Baldwin that the young man thought highly of himself and enjoyed strutting around as if he owned the place.

"Now, let's start again, shall we? Tell me, what the hell is going on?" Baldwin sat on the corner of the desk, looking at the ten TV screens attached to the wall in front of him, each showing a different area of the chateau and its grounds.

"The limos called in a few minutes ago. They got held up a few miles up the road. They should be here any minute," Benji said.

"Make sure they are. I'm getting anxious, and I don't need to tell you what that means, do I?"

The men nodded their understanding of the unspoken threat. Baldwin's anxiety was notorious, and it often resulted in bouts of violence. Despite his men having muscles ten times larger than their

IQs, when Baldwin went on the rampage, he knew they all turned into quivering wrecks.

With the threat still lingering in the air, Benji pointed to one of the screens as a car pulled into the drive. "Here comes the first lamb now."

Relieved, Baldwin headed for the door, but he stopped in the doorway, turned, and issued a final warning: "Remember what I said… Any fuck-ups, and I'll personally cut off your balls and serve them to the pigs."

Re-entering the Great Room, Baldwin clicked his fingers and the band brought the room to life with one of his all-time favourite Jazz numbers.

Julio gathered the girls together to make sure they understood their roles for the evening. Several of the girls noisily smacked on their gum, no doubt bored of hearing the same instructions for the fifth time since arriving mid-afternoon. The plans were embedded in their minds already. Baldwin made a mental note which of the girls he would punish later for showing Julio attitude.

An English butler announced the arrival of the guests as they entered through the main doors. "Mr. Chang Foo, representing the Chinese Government."

As each guest was announced, Baldwin stepped forward, a welcoming smile lighting up his handsome face. He lost his annoyance at their lateness—temporarily, at least.

"Mr. Yashicotin, representing the Japanese Government," the butler announced. After the dignitary shook hands with Baldwin, one of the young girls latched onto the man and guided him in the direction of the free bar at the rear of the room.

When everyone was assembled and the room was buzzing with excited chattering, Julio gave the signal for his men to take up their positions. The men who'd accompanied the limos drifted through the crowd and slotted into their allotted places around the room, roughly six feet apart, with their weapons still concealed.

As per their instructions, the band stopped playing as soon as Baldwin appeared on the makeshift stage. The room erupted with loud applause as he stepped up to the microphone. "Good evening, gentlemen. First of all, let me tell you what a great honour it is to welcome you into my humble home." Baldwin paused to accept the rapturous applause generously given by the audience, before he continued with his sucker-punch: "It has always been my ambition to become the world's richest man, and now, with the help of you and your respective governments, I'm in a position to achieve that ambition."

He noticed several of the brighter men in the group eyeing him with caution. Their unease changed to alarm as his men took out their guns.

"Now, now, gentlemen, settle down. There really is no need to be alarmed." Baldwin addressed the audience in a sing-song voice. "Providing, of course, you co-operate."

The Russian Finance Minister, his face flushed and contorted with rage, approached the stage. He gesticulated with his hands and shouted in his native tongue.

Outraged by the man's rudeness and the mistimed outburst, Baldwin nodded to one of his men standing nearby and signalled for the man to be silenced.

Three shots echoed around the room, and the Russian groaned.

Again, the Great Room fell silent.

The Russian clutched his chest and fell to the floor, his blood quickly making a pool beside him.

Several guests tried to escape out onto the terrace, but the armed men herded them back into the centre of the room.

Baldwin's calm, yet assertive voice rose above the commotion. "Gentlemen, you disappoint me. I thought we were all getting along so well. It's unfortunate that our Russian friend chose to disrespect me, but I hope the rest of you will learn from his mistake. The ball— as they say, gentlemen—is in your court. Now, what is your decision? Am I to take it from your silence the rest of you have no objections to helping me fulfil my ambition or—"

The Chinese Finance Minister chose to interrupt his speech. Yet another communist with balls, Baldwin thought, as the man approached the stage. Foo mumbled, "Robert, we are all friends here. We should discuss your ambition openly and frankly."

Baldwin's smile vanished. The Chinese Minister, whose position gave him great power, shrivelled in front of Baldwin. "And what do you foresee the outcome being, Mr. Foo?" Baldwin asked through clenched teeth.

Foo's body trembled. He tried to take a step back, but Julio's Colt dug into the base of his back. Panicked the man ran, but three shots prevented him from going more than a few paces. Foo cried out in agony and slumped as the impact of the bullets sent him sprawling to the newly polished floor, like a puppet whose strings had been cut.

"Is anyone else going to interrupt me? Speak now. My patience is wearing thinner by the minute."

The room remained silent.

Baldwin's triumphant laughter echoed round the enormous room as he sensed his long-awaited objective about to finally materialise.

Chapter Two

Lorne stretched and turned over to cuddle Henry, her Border collie. "Time to get up, lazybones."

Henry raised his head, stuck out his tongue, and licked the side of her face.

"What woman needs a man, when a dog can give kisses as good as that?" She gently nudged the dog off the side of the bed. Before going downstairs she walked into the bathroom and let out an agonised moan. "Christ, look at the state of me. What bloody man would consider sleeping with me anyway?" She studied the state of her makeup-smudged face and the way her shoulder-length brown hair stuck out.

Her eight-year-old dog whimpered in response, she suspected more out of desperation to relieve himself than in reply to her daft question. "Okay, mate. Come on."

She led the way down the stairs of her tiny two-bed terraced house in Highbury, with Henry trailing behind her. As Lorne unlocked the back door to let her faithful companion out, her eyes drifted up to the Arsenal wall clock hanging in her galley kitchen: Eleven fifteen. "Bloody hell. Where the heck did the morning go?" she mumbled, looking at the clock her dead partner had given her several years before.

Detective Sergeant Pete Childs had been Starsky to her Hutch, back in the days when she'd been a successful Detective Inspector in the Met, and he had been her partner, a friend whom she still missed daily. Now he was gone, gunned down in an alley by the Unicorn, the terrorist who'd become her arch-enemy over the eight years she'd hunted him. She'd come close to capturing him several times, only to have him escape when she thought he'd been cornered. She blamed the Unicorn for ruining her life.

The man had intentionally set out to teach her a lesson by kidnapping and raping her beautiful thirteen-year-old daughter, Charlie, and by putting Charlie to work in one of his seedy brothels alongside dozens of Eastern-European teenagers, smuggled into England in the backs of lorries. He'd also robbed her of the man for whom she had intended to her husband Tom.

Within days of burying her partner, she'd been forced to endure the unenviable task of repatriating pathologist Jacques Arnaud's body back to France, so his loving family could bury him. It was a job that had left her with a gaping hole in her heart.

That had taken place a little over a year ago, and the farewell to Jacques proved to be the final straw in tearing apart her career. After watching the Unicorn's boat blow up in a massive explosion, Lorne's DCI had insisted the criminal had carried out his last evil deed. But Lorne's instincts came into play and, as they watched the smoke billowing over the marina, she remained convinced the Unicorn, otherwise known as Baldwin, had managed to escape the blaze.

Whilst the DCI and the superintendent had been busy congratulating themselves and patting each other on the back for a job well done, Lorne had written out a two-page letter of resignation. She hadn't given DCI Roberts the chance to talk her out of it, either. After handing him the envelope, she had turned on her heel and walked out of the building and had never stepped back in the place since. She didn't even know if her superior had wanted to keep her as part of his team. That question still remained unanswered, as he'd never once bothered to contact her. It hadn't caused her sleepless nights, but it had pissed her off, just a little. In the end, she'd put his unwillingness to beg her to return to his team down to his enlarged ego.

Being as stubborn as he was, she would almost certainly have thrown his offer back in his face. Still, it wouldn't have hurt him to have asked.

Baldwin's final words visited her daily, too. *Each and every one of your loved ones will die.* And because of his callous, heartless threat—which, from him, was more of a promise—Lorne had divorced her husband Tom and forced her daughter to live with her father, out of harm's way. Her already fragile heart almost packed in at that point, not because of her divorce, but because it dawned on her she wouldn't be around to see Charlie flourish into a dynamic young woman.

Tom had insisted the proceeds from selling the house should be split down the middle fifty-fifty. However, with Charlie being raised by her father, Lorne had assured Tom that a sixty-forty split in his favour would be more than fair. Not wishing to argue any longer—

their whole marriage had been one big argument, anyway—Tom had the documents drawn up in a fifty-fifty split at the solicitor's without her knowledge, and the matter was closed.

Charlie's therapist applauded Lorne's decision to let her daughter live with Tom, believing it to be a more stable upbringing for the confused child. So, there Lorne was, all alone, with just Henry to keep her company through the long days and even longer nights. Her heart ached from everything she had been through in the past twelve months, and she prayed now and then for some way to get her life back on track.

Even Henry eyed her with sympathy during her rants of self-pity, when she wondered if she would ever get involved with a man again, if she could bring herself to put another person's life in jeopardy, with Baldwin at large. More often than not, she turned to a bottle of vodka for comfort.

The sound of Henry barking at the back door wanting to be let in pulled her out of her self-absorption. She opened the door just as the telephone in the lounge started to ring. "Stay there, mister. The last thing I want is you traipsing through the house with muddy paws. I'll be right back to dry you."

She hurried through the kitchen door, swiftly closing it behind her, blocking the dog's escape route. Lorne grunted as she hunted for the portable phone. "Where the bloody hell is it?" She tossed the scatter cushions lying on the couch to the far side of the room and finally found the phone. "Who is this? And what do you want?"

"It's a pleasure speaking to you too, Lorne," A deep velvet voice mocked.

"I repeat, who is this?" The voice sounded familiar, but her hangover prevented her from putting a name to it.

"You're a mighty difficult person to track down, even for someone with my exceptional skills." His sentence ended with a self-deprecating laugh.

"All right, buster, you've got exactly three seconds to tell me who you are, or I'm putting this phone down. One…two…"

"Jesus, woman! When did you lose your sense of humour?"

"Three." Lorne disconnected the call and stomped back to the kitchen, infuriated by both her inability to place the voice and the knowledge that she would never have had such a problem a year ago, when she'd been on top of her game. She needed sustenance to counteract her hangover blues.

She almost made it to the kitchen door when the phone rang again. Convinced that it would be the obnoxious caller ringing back, she found herself with a dilemma: Did she let the confounded phone just ring, in the hope he'd finally get the message and give up; or, for the sake of her sore head and the thought that she should know the caller, did she answer it a second time? "What the fuck do you want? I'm tired, hung over, and in no mood—"

"Lorne. For Christ's sake, it's Tony."

"Tony?"

"Oh, how easily the lady doth forget," the caller mocked.

"Enlighten me, then."

"I despair, really I do, Lorne. And there I was thinking we were good friends."

"I'm counting again; you know what will happen when I get to three. One…two…"

"Tony Warner, your friendly secret agent. Remember now?" Tony asked, his humour disappearing along with his patience.

After several seconds of quiet, Tony had to ask if she was still there.

"Yeah, I'm here. But why?" Lorne asked, collapsing into the sofa behind her.

"Why am I ringing you, you mean?"

"Yes?"

"If I said I'm checking in to see how you are, would you believe me?" he asked.

"That's a negative."

"That's what I thought. So, why don't you open your front door, let me in, and we can discuss why I'm getting in touch after all this time."

"You're *what*? You're here. But—"

The doorbell rang.

Lorne flung open her front door, forgetting she looked a mess, then watched in horror, as he took in the sight of her dressed in bubblegum pink pyjamas covered in comical penguins. Both of them had a phone pressed to the ear.

"Nice outfit. I must've missed that particular number at the London fashion show. Hi, Lorne. It's good to see you, kind of."

The more her cheeks burned, the wider the grin spread across his handsome, slightly scarred face.

Her mouth hung open for several moments before she grabbed

him by the collar and hauled him in through the front door.

"I think it's a little late to be concerned about what the neighbours might think, don't you?" he asked, laughing as he followed her up the narrow hallway.

"Wise arse. Give me a minute to throw on some proper clothes, will you?" Her cheeks were surely the colour of beetroot, and she hated herself for colouring up like that.

"Don't bother changing on my account. It's been a while since I've laid eyes on a young lady in such fetching jimjams."

As Lorne ran up the stairs, momentarily forgetting about the delicate state of her head, she gave him the finger behind her back. "Make yourself at home. Just don't go in the kit—" She stopped shouting mid-sentence when she heard Henry bounding up the stairs to find her.

"Sorry, did you say something?"

Shaking her head, Lorne grabbed the dog by his collar and dragged him into the bathroom so she could clean his dirty paws.

"Come on, mate. I know it's not your fault. If men had bloody brains, they'd be far too dangerous for this universe, or the next." With dog and owner both looking more presentable, they headed back downstairs to see what the deal was with their unexpected guest.

She found Tony standing by the kitchen window gazing out at her tip of a garden. "Work in progress, I guess you'd call that, huh?"

"If you must know, Tony, I've only just completed renovating this place. If you knew anything at all about property development, you'd know the last piece of the puzzle is always the garden and any external work."

"Is that what you are nowadays, a property developer?"

Lorne filled the kettle, feeling further embarrassed by the muddy footprints making not so pretty patterns across the newly tiled floor. "I was just about to dry Henry when you arrived, you'll have to excuse the mess in here—and throughout the rest of the house now, thanks to you."

"What did I do?" He sounded mystified, as only a man could, in such circumstances.

"Forget it. Why are you here?"

"Any chance we can go somewhere a little less messy?" Tony asked, his gaze on the kitchen table overflowing with dozens of interior design magazines and piles of unopened letters and bills.

Lorne poured the boiling water over the instant coffee granules and mumbled. "Cheeky sod." She added the milk and sugar, picked up the two mugs, and headed back up the hallway into the lounge at the front of the house. "This better?" she asked, handing one of the steaming mugs to the agent.

"Much. Now, I need you to sit down."

The humour had gone, and his expression looked more serious, which worried Lorne.

"You're kidding me. Just get on with it, Tony, for Christ's sake," Lorne snapped, refusing to take a seat on her comfortable new brown angled leather sofa.

"Sit."

As she met his troubled gaze, the hairs on the back of her neck stood to attention. His tone held a warning to expect the worst.

She took a step back and gently lowered herself onto the sofa, placing her mug on the side table beside her. "I'm sitting. Now, what's up?"

"He's back," Tony said.

Chapter Three

He's back! Two words. Two words that struck dread and fear into every pore of her skin.

Lorne felt the colour drain from her face, and her hands shook in her lap. She searched Tony's face and noticed the concern etched upon it. Even Henry, who was now sitting in front of her and tilting his head first one way and then the other, appeared to sense the magnitude behind those two small, but powerful words.

"He can't be. Not again." Her words came out as a whisper.

"Sorry, love, but I wouldn't lie to you."

Lorne licked her dry lips. "Where? Why?"

"He's been spotted in France—Normandy, actually. It doesn't look good, Lorne."

"Why? I mean, why have you tracked me down and come here? How does this concern me?" She could see the torment lingering in his hazel eyes.

"I need your help."

Lorne thrust herself off the sofa and stood in front of him. "My help! You want my help? Are you *bloody* insane, Tony?" She watched the hesitation flicker in his eyes.

"I assumed you'd want revenge."

"Of course I want revenge. Who wouldn't? But don't you think this guy has destroyed me enough already? I can't believe you're asking me to get involved in this. I've already had one breakdown. I don't think I could cope with another."

"I had no idea."

"No, no one did. I did my darnedest to hide it from everyone. Why should you know about it…?" Her voice trailed off.

"I shouldn't have come. It was wrong of me to disturb you. Forgive me, Lorne." Tony's shoulders slumped, and he looked defeated, something she'd never known before. He turned to leave, but she spoke, drawing him back into the room.

"Eight years I chased the Unicorn. Eight bloody years. Don't you think it's about time someone else had a pop at the guy. Jesus! I can't believe you're here. I really can't." She started pacing between the cast iron black fireplace and the sofa, her mind exploding, fracturing into pieces it would take a lifetime to put back together. Finally stopping in front of the fireplace she berated him again. "After all I went through, how *dare* you have the audacity to seek me out. To 'invite me' to get involved in what I know will prove to be another fruitless mission."

"At least think about it. Don't make a hasty decision that you'll spend the rest of your life regretting—"

Lorne raised her hand to halt his speech. "Stop it. Stop right there, buster. Don't play that game with me. I repeat, you know what I went through—what Charlie, my *fourteen-* year-old daughter went through—at the hands of that lunatic. It's obviously all in a day's work in your line of business. Well, I've got news for you, buddy: losing my career, my marriage, my partner, and the man I love—in my book, that counts for a phenomenal amount of pain. More pain than you or anyone else could endure in a dozen lifetimes. It's inconceivable of you to think I haven't suffered enough at the hands of this guy. That you should come knocking on my door like this. I find it downright fucking insensitive!"

"You're probably right, on all counts. But I remember what you used to be like."

Lorne watched Tony take a sip of his almost cold coffee and screw up his nose. His gaze scrutinised her five-foot-five frame.

"Why you…you shit bag." She took two steps towards him and thrust out an arm to slap the supercilious look off his face.

He caught her wrist before she made contact. "That's as may be. But I'm a shit bag who's desperate to rid the world of an even greater shit bag! And I truly thought you would feel the same way. Guess I was totally wrong with that one, huh?"

"Get out!"

"If that's what you want, I'll leave, and you won't hear from me again. If that's what you really want! Although when the idea sinks in, and I'm long gone, I think you'll be kicking yourself that you missed the opportunity to bring this guy down. Still, it's your choice, hon. Just remember this is a one-time offer. If I leave here empty-handed, I won't be coming back in a hurry. I won't have time, love. I'll be busy organising my travel plans. I leave for France this evening, with or without you."

Despite Lorne's couldn't-care-less attitude, she found herself wondering if maybe Tony knew her better than she knew herself.

Chapter Four

Once he'd left her house, she had thought long and hard about his offer. Finally, after half an hour of soul searching, the temptation had proven too much for Lorne. She had hit the redial on her phone and told Tony to count her in.

It was close to midnight when the plane touched down at Charles de Gaulle airport. The flight had been quiet, both of them lost in their thoughts, but they were brought back to the present as the plane landed with a bump.

"It's this way," Tony said, tucking his arm through Lorne's. He guided her to the exit, and they got in the back of the waiting courtesy car that Interpol had laid on for them.

Lorne put up with Tony's manhandling because she was exhausted. She felt as though the day's events had been a whirlwind, and she had been carried along with no way to control things.

After Tony's *surprise* visit, the day had panned out like this: First, she had called her father, begging him to dogsit Henry for a few days. Second, she'd made one of the toughest calls she'd ever had to make in her life. Charlie had picked up on the first ring, giving Lorne little chance to think up a plausible excuse why she had to cancel their plans for the weekend—plans that had been arranged for the last month and had included an extra special surprise, an early birthday present for Charlie: a table at The Ivy for eight o'clock. Six months that table had been booked—six bloody months! *Jesus, Tony really does pick his moments, doesn't he?*

But Charlie hadn't kicked up a fuss, hadn't ranted like other teenagers or reacted like the old Charlie would have. Maybe the girl's frequent visits to the psychiatrist, Dr. Carmichael, were paying off after all. Instead, her daughter had calmly said, "That's okay, Mum. I understand. Maybe next weekend, huh?"

The way the teenager had accepted the situation, without any arguments, only made Lorne feel worse. She hated letting her daughter down, but she knew that if the trip led to Baldwin's capture, both she and Charlie would end up celebrating at The Ivy and dancing on the table with joy. Whatever happened, Lorne would bend over backwards on her return and make it up to her only daughter. If they had to wait another six to eight months to sample some of the—if not *the*—finest food in the Capital, then so be it.

Tony jabbed Lorne in the ribs, interrupting her thoughts. "Hey, you with me, Lorne?"

"Yeah, just thinking." She smiled despite her tiredness.

"About letting Charlie down?" He probed.

She nodded. "Amongst other things."

"Did you explain why you're coming to France?"

"No. That was the hardest thing of all, not being able to tell her the truth. She's made giant steps in her therapy. I thought if I told her the real reason behind my visit, it might set her back. I told her one of my oldest friends desperately needed my help."

"Well, that's certainly true." He grabbed her hand, raised it, and squeezed it tightly. "I couldn't have done this without your help, Lorne." He surprised her further by touching his lips to the back of her hand.

Lorne brushed the sentimental gesture aside, not wishing to give it a second thought. "You old smoothie. You sure know how to wrap a girl round your little finger, don't you?"

"Years of practice, I guess. We should be at the hotel soon. We're staying here in Paris tonight, and after an early breakfast—seven all right with you?" She nodded, and he continued, "Another car is due to pick us up at seven thirty, then we have a rendezvous lined up with a few Interpol agents. That part is all pretty hush-hush. Not sure what will happen from there, but I'm assuming they'll escort us to Normandy and Baldwin's new hangout."

Lorne studied the famous Paris landmarks whizzing past her window, and bent forwards to see if she could see the top of the Eiffel Tower. "I'm glad you've stopped calling him the Unicorn. It was such an unlikely name for the bastard."

"I know what you mean. 'Baldwin' seems so much nastier, much more in keeping with his character."

"Maybe."

Considering Interpol was footing the bill, the hotel they were booked into turned out to be far grander than Lorne had anticipated. One step down from swanky, in her tourist guidebook.

A bellboy showed them to their rooms, which were opposite each other on the fourth floor.

Tony appeared to hesitate at his door, and Lorne pretended not to notice. She smiled to herself, feeling awkward. *Please don't try coming on to me!* "Remember, breakfast is at seven on the dot. Good night, Lorne."

She closed the door and locked it behind her. A shudder swept through her. *What was that all about? Why is Tony being so nice? Of course he would be—he needs your help, you idiot.*

She chastised herself for looking for something that clearly didn't exist. Had the Paris effect hit her? After all, it was supposed to be the most romantic city in the world. But she had no interest in Tony—or in any other guy, for that matter. When Jacques had died, she'd promised herself she'd never fall for anyone *ever* again. It was a promise she intended keeping. "Snap out of it, Lorne. You're tired and imagining things," she told herself as she began unpacking her overnight bag.

She cleaned her teeth in the en-suite bathroom and then settled into bed.

After half an hour of her mind refusing to switch off, she decided to call her father, back in London.

A groggy voice came on the line. "Yes, who is this?"

"Hi, Dad. It's me. Sorry to be calling so late, I just thought you might like to know that…I've arrived safely." She hesitated, then reprimanded herself for almost putting her foot in it. He had no idea she was even out of the country, let alone in Paris with a man. She'd told all her family she was visiting an old friend in Devon, alone.

"Lorne, sweetheart. Don't be daft. I dropped off in front of the box, that's all. I was waiting up for your call. How's Judith?"

"Umm, she's fine, Dad. She sends you her love. How's Henry settling in?" she asked, to quickly change the subject.

"He's fine. Well, that's a bit of a porkie, actually. The damn dog is driving me to distraction, keeps squeaking that damn toy of his, wants to bloomin' play all the time. The bloody mutt is wearing me out."

As if on cue, Henry squeaked his favourite toy in the background—not just once, but at least a dozen times. She laughed. "He loves ya, Dad. He knows when he sees you that you always play with him."

"That's when I come to visit you. I accept it then. But non-stop for twenty-four hours a day—that's a bit much, wouldn't you say?"

She could hear her dog growling and pictured her father trying to wrestle the "damn toy" off him. "Apart from that, is everything okay on that end?"

"Why wouldn't it be? You only left here a few hours ago, girl."

Because of her exhaustion, she'd managed to raise his suspicions. "Don't go getting all defensive on me. I was only asking." Lorne sidestepped her father's inquisition before it had the chance to get started.

"When did you say you'd be back?"

"Couple of days max, Dad," she lied, unsure what the actual timeframe would be for her visit.

Her father grunted. "I say the sooner you get back, the better, where this bloody dog of yours is concerned."

Lorne raised her eyes to the ceiling. "If he gets too much, Dad, maybe you can give Tom a ring. Perhaps he and Charlie can have him. I'm sorry, Dad; I thought the company might do you some good." His state of mind since her mother's passing two years earlier constantly worried her. Despite his daily assurance that he was coping well, the evidence to the contrary was overwhelming. His garden had gone from an award-winning entrant in the national garden scheme's "yellow book" to resembling Lorne's own shabby, unkempt plot.

"Now, don't start all that nonsense again, Lorne. If I've told you once, I've told you a thousand times: I'm all right. Granted, I'm no spring chicken, but given my age, I don't think I'm doing so bad."

She imagined him thrusting his shoulders back, pulling the natural curve out of his spine as he spoke. "All right, Dad. Whatever you say. I'm going to say good night now, if that's okay? You know I'm not the best traveller in the world. Good night, Dad. Give Henry a kiss from me."

"I'll do no such thing, you foolish woman. The trouble is you treat that dog like a bloody human. You know what that Cesar Millan says—you know that *Dog Whisperer* chap—he says they should know who is boss and shouldn't be treated like babies. But do you listen? Heck, you see every damn programme, and it still goes in one ear and out of the other—'

"Dad. I said good night. I'm going to hang up now, before we fall out."

Her father grunted again, before grudgingly saying good night to his beloved elder daughter.

Lorne shook her head, turned off the bedside light—the only accessory in the sparsely decorated room—and snuggled down under the duvet.

Despite her exhaustion, sleep evaded her for hours. In spite of her best efforts, her thoughts turned to Robert Baldwin and the people he'd stolen from her. Jacques, in particular. The irony of the situation hadn't passed her by, either, as she found herself in Paris without him by her side. It was ironic and unfair—but then, that just about summed her life up, didn't it?

Ironic and unfair!

Chapter Five

When the travel alarm her father had given her filled the room with more noise than its size suggested it was capable of, Lorne woke abruptly and banged the button to turn it off. Her eyes had trouble focusing.

The last time she'd looked at the clock had been at five fifteen. *Wow! A full hour and a quarter of sleep!*

Lorne tried to stretch out the knots resulting from sleeping in a strange bed, but her body refused to respond. It creaked and groaned as much as the bed itself. She slapped herself around the face a few times. "Come on, Lorne. Wake up. There's places to go and people to see." She threw back the duvet and headed for the bathroom.

Half an hour later, dressed in jeans and a jumper, she entered the hotel's dining room. Tony was already tucking into his breakfast at a table in the centre of the room. She pulled out the chair opposite and sat down. When she looked at his plate and noticed the size of his breakfast, her stomach clenched uneasily.

"Sleep well?"

"Does it look as though I have?"

He looked up, took a brief look at her, shook his head, and tucked into his meal again. "Sorry. Anyway, I've ordered you a full English. Hope you don't mind. There's no telling when we'll get to eat again, and as this is on Interpol's expense account, I thought we should make the most of it."

"Thanks, but no thanks. For a start, I don't over-indulge first thing; and for another, aren't you in the wrong country for a full English?" Lorne looked around the pleasantly decorated dining room, purposefully avoiding watching Tony stuff his face faster than some people could finish a glass of water.

"You could do with fattening up, Lorne," he said through a mouthful of sausage.

"Meaning?"

"Meaning you've lost a hell of a lot of weight since I last saw you."

"And?" She scowled.

"And, it ain't healthy. Dare I say you look scrawny? Borderline anorexic, even."

"Don't be so ridiculous. You're talking out of your backside. It's called hard work and exercise. You want to try it sometime? Might help get rid of your double chin." She reached across the table and tickled him under the chin and made the excess flesh wobble, emphasising her point.

"Really, Lorne. Joking aside, you need to put some pounds back on, hon."

A waitress appeared at the table and placed a plate in front of Lorne that was stacked as high as the Eiffel Tower they'd passed the day before. Lorne's eyes grew wide, almost popping out of her head at the amount of food she was expected to eat. She looked up at the girl. "I'm sorry. I just can't eat this. Can I have a croissant and orange juice instead?"

The waitress smiled, shrugged her shoulders, and left the table empty-handed. Lorne wondered if she'd seen amusement in the woman's eyes. "Um, excuse me. Just a minute…"

"Waste of time, Lorne. They don't speak the lingo. Just eat what you can—there's a good girl."

"Oh, is that right? Well, you seem to have found a way of being understood. Or maybe someone had a word with her, bribed her into pretending she didn't understand English. I recall seeing a documentary about France last year that reported the French people, both young and old alike, revel in showing off how much of our language they know. Funny, that!' Lorne poured herself a coffee from the *cafetière* sitting in the middle of the table and waited for him to answer.

"Whatever. Now, are you going to eat that breakfast, or am I going to have to force feed it to you? The punters round here won't mind. They're used to seeing that kind of thing. Instead of duck or goose foie gras, it'll be human, that's all."

"That's disgusting, and you wouldn't dare."

"The choice, as they say, is yours. Do I, or do *you*?"

Lorne picked up her knife and fork and reluctantly began tearing at a piece of shrivelled overcooked bacon.

"That's my girl. When we met last year, I knew you were a woman crying out to be handled firmly."

"Believe what you like, bully boy. What time are we due to meet with the Interpol agents?"

"At nine. Just enough time for another helping."

"You're kidding." Horrified, Lorne stared at her bulging plate and fought back the nausea threatening to surface.

"Yes, I'm kidding. Jeez, lighten up, will you? I don't recall you being so gullible."

Lorne pushed the food around the plate for another half hour and felt relieved when the car arrived to pick them up, giving her a reason to get away from her breakfast. With their overnight bags stored in its boot, the car set off through the rush hour traffic. Luckily, the head office of the National Gendarmerie was only a few kilometres away at *rue* St Didier in the XVI *arrondissement* of Paris, and their trip was over in next to no time.

The driver pulled up outside the building and flicked on his hazard lights. After walking them inside, he introduced them to the receptionist, bid them farewell, and then disappeared as swiftly as he'd driven them there.

Their ornate surroundings made Lorne gape, open-mouthed. The marbled columns stretched up like long limbs, reaching as far as the eye could see. Granite steps regally led up to several different galleried levels, and light streamed in from an enormous glass dome high above to flood the reception area.

"Pretty impressive, huh."

"That's one word for it, I guess." Lorne felt similar to how she thought Charlie must have felt the first time Tom and she had taken her to Alton Towers theme park.

"Ah, I see you are admiring our architecture, *monsieur, madame.*" The tall thin man wore a navy blue suit and a guarded smile. To the left of him stood a younger, fair-haired woman, who matched Lorne's height and build. She wore a suit cut in the same material as her male colleague.

The man's smooth velvet tone shocked Lorne for a moment. It was like listening to Jacques all over again. *Don't be so absurd, girl. You're in France. It's the way French people speak.*

"I am Capitaine Michel Amore from Interpol, and this is my colleague, Lieutenant Renée Levelle. You must be Monsieur Warner, but I feel at a disadvantage, as I am unaware of your name, *madame.*" He gave Tony's hand a firm shake and then surprised Lorne by shaking her hand limply. She detested a counterpart treating her differently, even more than she hated the thought of swallowing a live oyster. But then, she'd resigned a year ago, so she could no longer be described as his counterpart, could she?

"It's Lorne Simpkins, *capitaine*." She made a point of looking into his deep blue eyes and wondered if she'd spotted a look of recognition when she'd told him her name.

Tony spoke next and offered the reason for Lorne's inclusion on the case. "Lorne has been on the trail of this guy for the last eight years or so."

The *capitaine*'s shoulders straightened, and the smile disappeared from his rugged sun-tanned face. "Ah, Detective Inspector Simpkins, if I'm not mistaken."

"You've heard of me?"

"Oh yes, *madame*. You are—how do you say in English?—ah yes, notorious!'

Lorne shuddered, unnerved by the smirk that had appeared on the *capitaine*'s face. *What the hell does he mean by that, "notorious"?* She figured all would be revealed soon enough.

Chapter Six

The meeting finally drew to a close after an hour and a half, during which time Lorne hadn't uttered a word. No one had bothered to ask her opinion, and she had chosen not to volunteer anything. The only significant detail that the *capitaine* was willing to divulge about the ongoing case in France was that two men had been found murdered.

Arrangements were made for Lorne and Tony to head off to Caen, Normandy—the area where Robert Baldwin was said to be flaunting his wealth and power—straight after lunch.

As they approached the reception area again, Tony steered Lorne by the elbow, coming to a halt alongside one of the marble columns. "What the hell was that all about?" he whispered, as if hoping not to be overheard by the officers milling around them.

She wrenched her arm from his grasp. "I don't understand why you're so angry, Tony—or, for that matter, what the hell you're referring to."

"Jesus, what has gotten into you? Where's the spunky Lorne gone? A year ago, there's no way that bloke would've gotten away with disregarding you like that. What the fuck is going on?"

"If you don't like it, then I suggest you put me on the first plane home and let me get on with sorting out my garden, something I know I'm good at." She glared at Tony and felt the hairs on the back of her neck standing to attention.

Her voice had grown louder, attracting a lot of attention, and officers in uniform eyed them with suspicion. Tony hooked his arm through hers and led her out of the building. He spotted a café opposite and marched Lorne towards it. Tony ordered two *café au laits* while Lorne sat down. Joining her at the table, he demanded, "All right, you've got my attention and that of half the French National police. What gives, Lorne?"

She watched him shake his head in confusion. She felt confused by her own involvement and why Tony had brought her to France. "That man in there, the *capitaine,* implied that I don't belong here, and it got me thinking maybe he's right."

"We went through all this before we boarded the plane to come out here. *I* need you on this case with me. *I* need your expertise."

"The way I remember it, you turned up on my doorstep, and within a few hours I was flying to France. You didn't even give me time to think about it, Tony. You didn't give me a chance to say 'Get stuffed; I don't want to know.'"

"C'mon, Lorne, you know bloody well it wasn't like that."

He looked hurt, and she felt like biting her tongue off. He was right. It hadn't really been like that at all. It just felt good to turn the tables on him. "Anyway, what bloody "expertise'? You're far more experienced than I'll ever be. I resigned from all this crap, remember?"

"But why? Why all of a sudden, Lorne?"

"'All of a sudden'... You uncaring bastard. Maybe it dawned on me that life's too short to be constantly dealing with men who despise women, both coworkers and the criminals we try to bring to justice. I had to put up with shit from a particularly supercilious superintendent for years, a man who'd sooner walk the other way than say good morning to me. I see the same traits in Capitaine Amore. He made it perfectly clear in there that I had no place on this case. Maybe you're right in some respects; perhaps my feistiness has dwindled over the past year. I'm *'just'* a bloody housewife, Tony. Actually, I'm not even one of those. I'm one of the three million unemployed in Britain today."

"I can't believe we're having this conversation. You're nothing of the sort, Lorne. Why are you being so down on yourself?"

The waiter arrived with their coffees.

"I don't have to explain myself to *you* or anyone else. I've changed. Perhaps it took being involved in this kind of environment again to really thump it home to me. I don't *want*—or *need*—to be part of this kind of set-up anymore."

"Come off it, Lorne. Do I have to remind you about the conversation we had when we found your father after Baldwin had kidnapped him?"

"No." The word came out far sharper than she'd intended, but she wanted to stop him dragging up memories she'd fought for months to try to forget, the ones that prodded her conscience when she least expected it and filled her dreams when she actually managed to get any sleep.

"Well, that's tough, because I'm going to, anyway. Revenge, you swore that you'd get revenge."

Feeling like a teenager being reprimanded for shoplifting, she shrugged. "You know what they say, Tony: Words are cheap."

"That's right, and if anyone else had said that I might've believed them, but not you."

Out of nowhere tears welled up, and the cup she'd been gazing at became fuzzy. As she lifted her head to look at him, a tear slipped down her cheek.

He closed his eyes, which left her wondering if he regretted his harsh words. His hand slid across the table and covered hers.

"Lorne, come on. If I don't know what's going on in that pretty head of yours, I can't help you, can I?"

"Have you ever lost anyone you've loved, Tony? Truly loved, I mean?" She rotated her cup in its saucer as she watched the changing expressions flicker across his face.

"Yes and no," he said.

"When I say 'lost', I mean 'died'. Have you lost them from your life altogether?"

"No, I can't say I have. I know where you're going with this. You reckon I can't possibly understand what you're going through. That isn't the case, girl. In my line of business, the death of a colleague is a regular occurrence; and while I'm not saying you ever get used to it, I'm trying to make you understand that it makes you a stronger person. A much stronger person, one who adapts to living their own life in a more fulfilling way."

There was a moment's silence as she mulled over his words.

Tony spoke again, and that time his words arrowed in on the truth of how she felt about her life and what it had become. "You want to know what I see, Lorne? Well, you're going to hear it anyway." He paused long enough to reach over and lift her chin up. "I *totally* understand where you're coming from, babe, but now is the time to let go and to stop bloody feeling sorry for yourself. It's been a year, a whole year, since Pete and Jacques died. It's time to move on."

"That's a little simplistic even for you, don't you think?"

"You need to, love, for your own peace of mind, and for health reasons. I'm not here to lecture you, but looking at you, someone needs to give you a kick up the backside. Maybe you're feeling this way because the Unicorn is around again. Perhaps he has stirred up old feelings you thought were forgotten. What do you say? Do it for me, huh? Do it for Pete and Jacques up there." He pointed to the ceiling of the café. "Ask yourself this: If you were the one murdered by the Unicorn, do you think they would pass up the chance to get revenge?"

Could her need for revenge really undo the past? She shrugged her weary shoulders and nodded. "I guess not. I'm sorry to burden you with this, Tony. I feel such a fool."

"Hey, that's what friends are for, isn't it?"

"I promise from now on, I'll be a different woman. But how are we going to get over the fact that Capitaine Amore doesn't feel comfortable with me on the case?"

"You leave that side of it to me. And Lorne, welcome back, love. Now let's go catch ourselves a Unicorn."

Chapter Seven

Baldwin paced around the lounge, kicking and throwing things out of his way. "I won't say it again, Julio. The man's a fucking idiot, and I want rid of him."

"Boss, I'll deal with him. It was a mistake, that's all."

"'Mistake', my arse. The man is a liability. I said *deal with him.*" Baldwin saw the fear glint in Julio's eyes, and a surge of pleasure ran through him at the knowledge of his dominance.

"I'll see to it straight away, boss."

"Be sure to let the others see the outcome." Baldwin cut the end from a ten-inch Cuban cigar and lit it, signifying their conversation was over, but he sensed that Julio wanted to say more. "What?" he demanded.

"Just one more chance, boss. If we get rid of him, we'll be a man down; and at this late stage, we won't get the chance to find a replacement."

Baldwin stepped forward, blowing smoke in the other man's face. "Not trying to protect him are you, Julio?"

"No, boss, but—"

"But he *fucked* up. I gave clear instructions for how I wanted those bodies disposed of, and he couldn't even do that. Don't forget, he was the one who screwed up the flights last week, and he cocked up the vehicle exchange on the last job."

Julio opened his mouth to speak, but Baldwin gave him a sharp look, and he quickly closed it again.

Baldwin smiled when he saw the look of resignation register on the Spaniard's face, "You all know what the consequences are for failure... Now, get rid of him."

As Julio turned to walk out the room, his shoulders slouched, Baldwin added, "String him up from the tree in the courtyard, and don't forget to make sure the others witness it."

He turned and walked across the room to the French doors, throwing them open he inhaled the autumn fresh air, and a calmness he'd never before known washed over him. At forty-eight, he finally felt at home. He no longer needed to envy the filthy rich, because he had joined the elite club. The huge chateau—and the five million pound yacht anchored in the South of France—was evidence of that. "Living the dream"—yep, he certainly was, and his final venture would ensure that dream never slipped away. *And they say crime doesn't pay!*

The money had already started to trickle in, and in a month's time, he'd be known as the world's richest man.

* * *

Julio walked into the kitchen, where he found several of the men playing cards at the large oak table, a basket of croissants and *pain au chocolat* in the centre. One look at his face, and the men knew something was wrong.

"Hey, what's up, Julio?"

With a heavy heart Julio explained to the four men what needed to be done. Without argument or hesitation, the group threw down their cards and set off to find Benji. They found the prankster of the unit in an adjacent room, engrossed in a game on his PlayStation. Terry grabbed him by the scruff of his neck and hoisted him to his feet.

"Hey, what the fuck, Ter—"

Mario, Benji's brother, carried on playing as though nothing had happened.

"Mario, help me." But Mario remained glued to his seat, refusing even to make eye contact with his kid brother.

The four men dragged Benji through the back door and into the large gravelled courtyard. He thrashed out at those around him with his arms and legs, but his efforts proved pointless.

"Come on, guys. You've had your fun." He laughed nervously. "Let me go now, eh!'

Three of the men held on to their detainee while the fourth threw a thick rope, with a noose at the end, up and over one of the thickest branches of an old oak tree. Even the Arabian horses in the nearby stables sensed the man's plight and became restless.

The colour drained from Benji's face as he realised what was about to happen, and he turned to plead with Julio again. "Julio, mate, come on. It was a simple mistake, a mistake any one of us could've made. Tell the boss I'm sorry… Dock me a month's—no, a year's wages! It'll never happen again—come on, give me a break, man!"

Julio placed the noose around the twenty-six-year-old's head, pulling the rope tight. In a strained voice, laced with regret, he said, "I'm sorry, Benji, but you royally fucked up, mate. I've tried, believe me, but you know what happens when the boss has made up his mind. Take your punishment quietly; take it like a man."

Before Julio could back away, Benji spat in his face.

To Julio's surprise, Mario grabbed the rope from the guy holding it and hoisted his brother off the ground.

After Benji's neck snapped, silence hit the courtyard. No more screaming. No more pleading. Just silence. They watched the body swing in the breeze for a few minutes before Mario stepped forwards to lower his brother's body to the ground. Without saying a word, he made a sign of the cross and stared down at his brother's body.

"I tried, Mario. I pleaded with him to let Benji live. We all know what we signed up for here. Benji was a fool, to forget about this. Don't be an arse and follow in his footsteps." Julio placed a comforting hand on the man's huge shoulder.

Mario shrugged the hand off and turned to Julio, his eyes blazing with contempt. "I will avenge my brother's killing one day—of that you can be certain, Julio. I chose to kill him out of respect. I didn't want any of you scumbags doing it. He would've understood that. But be warned, my friend, you'd better watch your back."

Mario strode back into the house with the other men close behind him, while Julio remained where he was and watched them go.

Chapter Eight

Lunch for Lorne consisted of half a baguette, filled with Camembert cheese and roasted ham, washed down with a bottle of Panache. Tony hadn't wanted to hang around the hotel twiddling his thumbs and waiting for Interpol to get their arses into gear, so he insisted they should take in at least one of the tourist attractions Paris had to offer. Of course, he'd opted for the cheapest one, a leisurely stroll along the Seine with a picnic lunch bought from a nearby patisserie.

"I must say, Tony, you sure know how to show a girl a good time." Lorne teased, sounding and feeling far more relaxed than she had in ages despite not knowing what lay ahead of them. She laughed as Tony's hand shot up to his chest as if he'd been mortally wounded.

"And you, dear lady, know how to hurt a man. What more could a woman want out of life? To be wined—well, lagered, actually, but that's by the by. As I was saying: to be wined and dined by the side of the river, in the city of lurrrvvveee."

"Idiot." Lorne laughed again and poked him in the leg. It felt strange to hear her own laughter filling her ears, but at the same time it felt good too, and it had certainly been a long time coming.

"That's better."

The relief on his face sent a pang of guilt through her for burdening him with her problems.

"We better head back soon." Tony smiled at her.

"What time did you say we're due to leave?"

"Around two. It's compulsory in France to have a two-hour lunch, from twelve to two. It's not as bad as it used to be. I came here on an assignment about ten years ago, and literally everything came to a standstill at that time. It doesn't seem quite so bad now."

"Does that mean it's followed by a siesta—you know, like in Spain?"

He laughed. "I don't think the French have quite reached that stage, yet."

"Christ, they don't know they're born. The way my working life panned out, most days I barely managed to fit in half a sandwich, and often I had to bolt that down while filling out paperwork, urgent paperwork needed by someone as equally stressed out as me. I guess it just shows what mugs we are back in England, huh! I bet it's the same in your line of business?" Lorne hoped the agent would open up a little in their relaxed surroundings. She knew very little about what made him tick, and even less about his personal life.

"Your assumption is first-class, as usual, Lorne." He swivelled on his heel to set off in the opposite direction. "Come on; let's get a shift on."

"A man of few words, aren't you, Tony? One could almost say you're a man of mystery."

"Goes with the territory. You of all people should know that."

"Talking of which, what's the game plan for this afternoon?" For a moment, she paused on the embankment to watch the boats, large and small, bobbing on the river. In the distance, a few large tourist boats could be heard, giving their passengers the usual blurb about their location, in both French and English.

"In what respect?"

"You know, with Capitaine Amore. It's obvious the guy doesn't want me hanging around, not that he doesn't have a point, I'm guessing this is probably the first time an ex-Met Inspector has turned up on his patch expecting to be involved in a case."

"Leave him to me. I did some background checks on him in my hotel room last night."

"You did? And?"

"He seems more than capable. He's been a copper since leaving school, been decorated by the president himself for capturing several dangerous criminals. He's the guy who has been entrusted with the daunting task of tracking down thirty-four thousand pieces of stolen art."

"You're kidding. This art, was it all stolen here in France?"

"No, all over the world. He spends a lot of his time working for Interpol. Apparently they have a file that is updated regularly and circulated to every known buyer in the trade, as well as museums, auction houses, police, and customs in every country."

"If that's true, then why is he involved in the Unicorn/Baldwin case?" she asked.

"Think about it, Lorne."

They remained quiet for the remainder of the walk, then finally Lorne's brain cells merged, and her mind sparked into life. *My rustiness for the job sure shows.* "I get it. Baldwin's been a naughty boy and stolen some paintings. He's branching out into yet another deceitful field."

Tony smiled, evidently amused at how long it had taken Lorne to suss everything out, and shook his head. "Not just paintings, Lorne. Different forms of art, anything with a hefty price tag. Sculptures, paintings—in fact if it comes under the art genre, then you can guarantee the Unicorn will want a piece of the action."

"Christ, is there ever anything that guy refuses to get tangled up in?"

"Yeah," Tony said, straight-faced. "Anything that's legal!"

Chapter Nine

They set off on time, at exactly two fifteen, with Lieutenant Levelle behind the wheel and Capitaine Amore sitting in the passenger seat for the two hundred and thirty-kilometre drive to Normandy. Their trip would have been a pleasant one, if only the car hadn't been filled with an awkward silence. The landscape surrounding them reminded Lorne of childhood family summer holidays spent in the depths of the beautiful Devonshire countryside.

The *capitaine* finally broke the silence, turning in his seat to look at Lorne. "Ah, I see our countryside brings joy to your face, Madame Simpkins."

Her smile vanished. *How the hell could he see me?* She noticed the small mirror in the pulled down sun visor, which answered her question. How long had he been watching her? More to the point, *why* had he been watching her? *In for a penny in for a pound. If I have to work with this guy, there's no harm in being civil to him.* "The countryside is very similar to where I used to visit when I was a child. I guess it's hard not to reminisce."

"Let me guess: Your childhood was spent in Devon, yes?"

How on earth did he figure that one out? She tried to suppress her surprise but found it difficult to prevent her amazement showing. *Maybe he's a bloody clairvoyant in his spare time!*

Before she could respond, he let out a full belly laugh. "I am from around here, and as a young boy, I heard many English people say the same thing."

Further surprised, she lifted a brow. "Oh, I see."

Awkward silence filled the car again. Lorne found it hard to put her finger on how she felt; the *capitaine* appeared to be something of an enigma; she didn't know what to expect from him next.

After travelling for nearly two and half hours they pulled up outside their hotel, located in the centre of town, a few metres past the magnificent and extremely imposing Caen cathedral.

"We will rendezvous again at seven for dinner," the *capitaine* informed them.

Lorne pulled Tony to one side. "I don't have anything to wear, Tony." Could the trip possibly get any worse?

"Don't worry about it, Lorne. The French don't tend to dress up much for dinner. It'll be cool. You'll be fine with whatever you have."

After being allocated their rooms, all on the fifth floor, they went their separate ways.

In dire need of freshening up after their journey, Lorne ran herself a hot bath. As the bubbles tickled her skin, she rested her head against the back of the bath and thought about the evening ahead. She wondered which of the two *capitaines* would turn up at the restaurant: the obnoxious one, or the kinder one that had surfaced in the car.

After dressing in a fresh pair of jeans and her best T-shirt, she returned to the bathroom to apply her makeup, which she had already decided should be subtle and definitely not overdone. A knock at the door interrupted her. "Just a minute, Tony," she called out. "I'm in the middle of making myself look beautiful."

Still laughing at her little quip, she opened the door to find an amused-looking Lieutenant Levelle.

"Madame, you do not need to make yourself look more beautiful." The woman smiled. She was dressed in a tight-fitting cream top and a snug black pencil knee-length skirt. Her glossy long hair, which had been tucked up in a bun all day, hung loosely down her slender back.

"*Lieutenant*, this is a surprise. Am I late?" Lorne asked, gazing down at her watch.

"No, *madame*, you are not." She gave Lorne another faint smile. "I was wondering if I could have a private word with you, before you enter the lion's den."

Lorne raised an inquisitive eyebrow and opened the door wider, inviting the woman to take a seat on the end of her bed. Lorne perched her bottom on the small console table a few feet from the *lieutenant*. "Lion's den? Is that a French term for restaurant, or is it your intention to place fear into my heart? Please explain yourself, Lieutenant."

"Please, call me René while we are off duty, Madame Simpkins."

"Only if you agree to call me, Lorne."

René nodded, and smiled. "Lorne, I wanted to warn you, if you like." The young French woman said, her English not quite matching the fluency of her colleague's.

"Go on." Lorne crossed her arms in front of her.

"I just wanted to say that the *capitaine* means well."

"I'm afraid I don't understand. In what respect?"

René coughed self-consciously before going on. "He comes across as a man without a heart, but it is a façade. Underneath he is... How you say? A real pussycat."

"Forgive me if I seem a little stupid, but I don't really understand why you've taken it upon yourself to visit me, Lieutenant."

"I am sorry, Lorne, if you think I am speaking out of turn, but I wanted to tell you that the *capitaine*, myself, you, and Agent Warner are all singing from the same hymn sheet. Is that how you say it?"

Lorne realised the woman's intention was to keep the peace among the four of them. Maybe her visit was intended as a diplomatic mission? Relaxing, Lorne laughed and told the *lieutenant*, "Actually you call the *capitaine* a pussycat; in my book, he'd give a Bengal tiger a run for its money."

Both women laughed, and Lorne could tell that they were indeed trying to sing from the same hymn sheet.

Lorne excused herself and stepped back into the bathroom to clean her teeth. After taking a last look at her under-dressed appearance, she returned to the bedroom, where her uninvited guest was sitting watching her. Lorne glanced down at her outfit, held her hands out to the side, and apologised. "It'll have to do, I'm afraid. Agent Warner gave me little time to pack, and I didn't anticipate dining out."

"Nonsense, Lorne, you look fine," the *lieutenant* said, as they headed for the door. "I am sure the *capitaine* will be pleased by what he sees."

Lorne inwardly questioned the woman's response, wondering if she meant what the comment implied.

Chapter Ten

The "pussycat" and Tony were already seated at the table, and as the two women weaved their way through the empty tables, Lorne sensed someone watching her. She shrugged the feeling away. *What is this guy's problem?* Sensing the *capitaine* to be the cause of her discomfort, she made a conscious effort to avoid eye contact with him.

"Madame Simpkins." The *capitaine* held out the chair for her, bowing he added, "May I say how lovely you look tonight?" He gave her a smile she had trouble deciphering.

You can say it, buster. Whether I believe you is another matter entirely! "Thank you."

"We shall order drinks and our food before discussing our likely strategy." The *capitaine* announced, making sure they all knew he was in charge of proceedings, whether they were on or off duty.

The two French officers ordered typically French cuisine, escargots served in garlic butter, followed by duck a l'orange, while Tony surprised her by ordering his food in excellent French. He explained that he ate out a lot in restaurants and only understood culinary French. The *capitaine* appeared both pleased and impressed; he stared at Tony and nodded. Lorne, however, struggled with the menu. After a while, she plumped for the *coq au vin*, the only dish she could read and understand.

The *capitaine* laughed. It helped ease the tension around the table. "Madame Simpkins, I see you are a very independent person. If you could not read the menu, you should have asked for some advice."

"It's Lorne, and I didn't want to put anyone out. Anyway, if you had ordered for me, I sense I would have ended up with some unthinkable part of an animal, such as a pig's head!'

"So to me it is clear you do not trust us. Instead, you ordered the safest thing on the menu."

"Ah, I see you French men have a problem with strong independent women." She looked over at Tony, who shook his head, his eyes pleading with her to shut up. "It must be a force thing; the Met hate strong women, too." She noticed Tony cringe and realised she'd overstepped.

The *capitaine* laughed. Instead of being pissed off by her stubborn words, he appeared to be amused by them. *Is he laughing with me or at me?* "I see I have found an equal in you, Lorne. It surprises me that you are no longer a police officer. Your attitude would be a considerable advantage."

His expression turned serious, and Lorne wondered if his backhanded compliment had been intended.

"Times change, I guess. People change, *Capitaine*."

"That they do, Lorne. And in your circumstances, I can understand why you chose to turn your back on the law. You must feel let down by your colleagues, *non*?"

Her eyes narrowed. "My circumstances?"

"With this Robert Baldwin—the Unicorn, if you will. I've read the dossier on what this scoundrel—as you English say—did to your friends and family."

His words shook Lorne. She didn't believe his insensitivity was intentional, but that was how it came across. She barely knew the man, and yet there he was, talking about the raw subject that had almost destroyed her life a year ago, and doing so as though they were discussing something as trivial as the weather.

Feeling cornered, she glanced over at Tony for help, but he and the *lieutenant* were too caught up in their own conversation to notice her discomfort. Her uneasiness grew, and she suddenly began to feel isolated and trapped, like a deer on a country road frozen in the headlights of an approaching car.

She sipped her glass of water and searched for an adequate response to the *capitaine*'s probing. *Get a grip girl, he meant nothing. You're looking for problems that simply aren't there.*

As if sensing he'd made her feel uncomfortable, the *capitaine* leaned over and whispered, "If I have offended you, Lorne, I am truly sorry."

She placed her glass back on the table and looked up at him. She studied his blue eyes and thought she saw compassion lingering deep inside. He smiled, a smile that made her think she'd misjudged him. Her powerful sixth sense prodded her conscience, and for some unknown reason, she felt a bond of trust had formed between them.

When she didn't respond to his apology, he leaned towards her again and whispered, "Has the cat got your tongue—is that the phrase you English use?"

Lorne shrugged. "I guess I'm a little confused!"

"Confused—yes, that is understandable. You come to our country, and I must admit I did little to welcome you. You must forgive me for my previous aggression towards you. I read the dossier about your horrendous ordeal only in the past few hours." Leaning in again so the others at the table could not hear, he whispered, "I knew Jacques Arnaud."

Those last words hit Lorne the hardest. Her eyes grew wide and instantly misted up. Lost for words, she stared at the *capitaine*.

"Forgive me, Lorne, for digging into old wounds. But you see we have something very much in common."

"We do?" Lorne whispered, as images of her darling Jacques filled her mind, and the usual pain tugged at her heart.

"Revenge. *Chère madame*, revenge. Believe it or not, he was a good friend of mine. We began our careers at the same time and kept in contact. Even when Jacques moved to London, we never lost contact." He smiled, and Lorne could tell he was reminiscing.

Her heart pounded, and she felt compelled to ask. "Oh, my God… Did he ever mention me when you spoke to him?"

He shook his head. The hopeful smile slipped from her flushed face, and she could tell the next words he spoke were supposed to raise her dipping spirit. "He did not mention you by name, but he told me he had found someone special, and that it was complicated. I presumed that person was married; he insisted that he was prepared to wait for her because she was so special."

Had fate sent the *capitaine* her way? Maybe Jacques had sent him to help her avenge his death.

Lorne nodded. "I understand. I was married at the time. We were due to meet…to discuss a future together. I had decided to leave my husband." For some strange reason she felt she owed the *capitaine* an explanation for the way his good friend had died. She continued, "I thought Jacques had changed his mind when he neglected to turn up, but then my phone rang. It was Jacques; he sounded scared. I thought he'd had second thoughts about our relationship, but the…the phone was snatched away from him, and the Unicorn— Baldwin—came on the line. He was holding him hostage—that's a speciality of his. He takes hostages in order to achieve his goals. Anyway, the Unicorn taunted me for a bit, and then I heard two shots, the *bastard* told me Jacques was dead." Much of her inner strength had died the minute she'd heard those shots that fateful day.

She hadn't realised it, but as she recounted the devastating events the way they had unfolded tears had started streaming down her face, and her voice had risen in anger.

The dining room had grown quiet as her voice cut across the other diners' conversations. Lorne saw pity written on the other diners' faces.

Tony nudged her with his elbow. "Are you all right, Lorne?"

Ashamed, Lorne bolted from the room and caught an empty elevator.

As the elevator rose to the fifth floor, she studied her reflection in the mirror. The recently applied mascara had left a thick gunky black trail through her foundation, and she dabbed at it with a tissue, but that only made it worse. "You idiot. Lorne, when are you going to learn to deal with this and move on with your sad life?" she asked out loud. When she didn't answer herself, she smiled in relief. At least her sanity was intact, kind of!

She sucked in her cheeks in frustration their evening plans had been destroyed by her willingness to wallow in self-pity, which needed to stop. She would call Tony later to apologise and to suggest that it would be best for them all if she returned to England, immediately.

Chapter Eleven

His "special" phone rang, interrupting his evening meal of *foie gras* and *beef bourguignon*. Baldwin answered it as he continued to pick at his rich food. "Yes?" He nodded, listening with interest to what the caller told him. "Very well. The usual amount will be deposited in your private account in the morning. *Merci, au revoir.*" He ended the call with the only French words he knew, the only ones he intended to learn.

Baldwin picked up and rang the little hand bell lying on the polished mahogany table beside him.

Julio entered the room a few seconds later. "Yes, boss?"

"There's been a development."

"Oh? So we'll need to adjust our plans."

"We leave first thing in the morning."

"Heading for where, boss?"

"That doesn't concern you. The pilot's the only one who needs to know my itinerary, got that?" Baldwin glared at his number two, and Julio nodded in response. "Now go. Get things sorted." He waved his hand to dismiss the Spaniard and tucked into his food again.

He had no intention of letting anyone know what his plans were. Since he'd ordered Benji's death, his men had been jumpy—jumpier than normal, anyway—the complete opposite of what he'd intended or expected. He could tell none of them were happy. He'd seen the loathing in their eyes, and yet none of them had said anything to him. For the first time he sensed this group of men, given the opportunity, wouldn't think twice about stabbing him in the back. He shrugged. *Am I bothered? Am I fuck!*

Within a month he'd be the richest man in the world, with or without his band of merry men. Muscles came and went like the seasons in games like his. If his current mob didn't work out, he'd kill them and find another group, one that was nastier and more respectful. He paid good money, and at the last recruitment day, no fewer than two hundred beefcakes had turned up hoping to get a job.

None of them had been put off by his unique interview method either. The "interviewees" were forced to take part in a gladiatorial-type battle, with the winner having the honour of joining his well-paid staff, while the loser ended up in a ditch somewhere with his throat cut. Survival of the fittest had definitely proved to be the order of the day.

The last two men to cock-up, apart from Benji, had been the men who'd led Lorne Simpkins to his planned escape route, Portsmouth Harbour. The day after they'd started their seven-year stretch for aiding and abetting a criminal in Pentonville Prison, guards had discovered them both hanging from the window bars of their cells, bed sheets wrapped around their throats and their guts leaving a bloody mess on the floor beneath them.

Baldwin had insiders on his payroll in every prison the length of Britain, just in case. He never knew when he might need one to carry out an inside job.

"Ah, Lorne Simpkins, now there's a name I know well. I wonder what she's doing on my tail. Last I heard, she was on the verge of a nervous breakdown." Baldwin laughed raucously before continuing his conversation with himself. "Now, if the chance arises, I have every intention of finding out what the little lady is made of. Sugar and spice—that's definitely not what her vixen of a daughter had running through her veins after I'd finished with her." He laughed again, then returned to his dinner, thoughts of how he'd treated Charlie running through his mind.

Baldwin intended his last planned venture to go out with a bang, and he couldn't think of a better way to do it than with his nemesis, Lorne Simpkins. He had been working on a plan for the past few months, which was why he had resurfaced in France, after allowing the world to think he was dead following the explosion at Portsmouth Harbour.

He knew she'd want revenge for him taking her lover's life. Well, the time had come to see what the former inspector was made of.

Chapter Twelve

Lorne had just drifted off to sleep when a knock at the door woke her. In a daze, she grabbed the hotel's white towelling robe out of the bathroom, threw it on, and opened the door.

The words tumbled out before she had a chance to stop them. "*Capitaine*…um. I'm sorry, bed I was in—I mean, I was just going to sleep."

She blushed as the *capitaine*'s eyes ran up and down her slim body. "I was worried about you, Lorne—concerned, even. Can I come in?"

Not knowing what else to do, she stepped to one side and welcomed her unexpected visitor, at the same time pulling the robe tighter, self-conscious about the T-shirt she was wearing as a nightdress. "I'll just throw on some clothes…"

He shook his head to interrupt her. "There is no need. You are quite safe, *madame*. I don't make a habit of jumping on pretty women—unless invited to, of course." He laughed, and she sensed it was to ease the awkwardness of the situation.

Lorne's blush deepened. "Glad hear to it." *Jesus, woman get a grip.* She shook her head and tried again. "I'm glad to hear it, *Capitaine*. Please, won't you sit down?" She pointed to the small pink dralon-covered stool under the console table, expecting him to sit there.

He surprised her by sitting on the bed, where he bounced up and down a few times. "I suspect this is more comforted than the bed in my room."

"Comfortable… You mean comfortable."

"Ah, sometimes I believe my English to be better than it actually is. Thank you for correcting me."

The smile slipped from his handsome tanned face, and Lorne feared she'd upset him. She'd often heard how temperamental French people could be, especially when corrected in their attempts to speak other languages. "I just wish my French was half as good as your English," she remarked, before changing her tone. "What are you doing here, *Capitaine*?"

"Ah, you are a direct woman. I like that. I am here to discuss the case with you. Please, join me." He patted the bed next to him, but she chose to sit on the dralon stool instead.

She winced, regretting her decision as a piece of broken wood concealed by the material jutted into her coccyx.

The *capitaine* laughed. "I'm guessing not as *comfortable* as the bed. Your choice, *madame*. As I was saying downstairs before I insensitively upset you, at first I was against your being here; but now that I have the full facts, I can only welcome your involvement. I was hoping—if it doesn't prove to be too painful for you, of course—you could run over the history you have with this Baldwin character."

"Surely all the facts are in the dossier you referred to, *Capitaine*."

"It's Michel."

Confused, she shook her head. "What is?"

"My name. Instead of *Capitaine*. When we are alone, it would be better for you to call me Michel."

"Oh, I see. Very well, Michel, again I refer you to the dossier."

"You can refer all you like, but you and I both know such dossiers only brush the surface of criminals such as this man. Put another way, I want the... How do you say it? The nitty gritty on this guy?"

Lorne nodded, finding it hard to keep a straight face at his terminology. "Your English is sometimes quite entertaining. Surely it would be better for me to look at the dossier to see what has been left out."

"I agree. If you wish, I could collect it from my room, but I fear it would be of no use to you. It is written in French, and you have already told me that your French is...very limited."

"I didn't think of that. Okay, let me start from the beginning. Please stop me if you don't understand anything." She crossed her legs, and the robe fell open. Embarrassed, she stood up and readjusted the material.

"I forgot you English have a reputation for being prudes. There is no need to do that on my account. So different to the women in my country, who are carefree with the amount of flesh they show—in a sophisticated way, of course."

Lorne chose to ignore the cultural jibe. "As I was saying, it was my misfortune to get involved with Baldwin approximately nine years ago. I must emphasise he is by far the worst criminal I ever had to deal with during my career in the Met. The lowest of the low.

'Murdering bastard' should be his middle names. Vice squad were the first to come across him; they received a tip-off about a drugs shipment due to arrive at Liverpool docks."

She paused, and Michel prompted her to go on. "At the time, their information was very limited. They had no idea where or when the shipment would arrive; the informant only knew it was 'imminent'. When the vice squad got to the scene, they found their informant hanging from a beam. His charred remains were still smouldering. The ports and airports were alerted immediately. There was one major problem, though: We didn't have a clue who this guy was. Actually, Tony Warner was the one who discovered the Unicorn's true identity only last year—you know, when…

"Anyway, like I said, we were completely in the dark back then. After the informant's body was discovered, two traffic cops pulled over a vehicle for speeding on the M62—that's a busy motorway in the North of England. The two officers left their vehicle, and as they approached the offending car, they were gunned down. They didn't stand a chance—you see, our regular police are unarmed. Unfortunately, my godson was one of the police officers. He'd just completed his training at Hendon; he'd only been on the streets for a few months." She stopped and looked up at Michel; his eyes glistened in the light. He nodded, encouraging her to continue with her story. "After that, my partner Pete and I came across the Unicorn a few times, but we could never get close enough to catch the slippery bugger."

Michel wrinkled his brow. "Slippery bugger?"

"Sorry, the bastard—that's a much more accurate name for him. The trouble is, he's the type of guy who doesn't mind going under the knife—you know, plastic surgery, facial surgery. Which is how he managed to avoid being identified all those years.

"Here's the thing, though: To ensure his new identity remained a secret, he always killed the surgeon after they'd operated on him. Like I say, he's a pretty brutal kind of guy. Anyway, we reckon because of greed, his activities escalated last year. He became involved in people trafficking and joined forces with a wealthy Russian billionaire called Abromovski."

Again, Lorne paused to see if the Frenchman was following her. He nodded, and she continued, "Together they set up brothels. High-class brothels, ones regularly frequented by well-known pillars of the community—MPs, judges, planning councillors. Their main objective was that they showed these guys a good time—at least, the girls did—in return for favours. In other words, extortion. The most despicable part of all this was they held regular auctions, where girls as young as twelve were sold to the highest bidder." Lorne fell silent as she reached the part of the story that personally involved her and her family.

With genuine concern touching his voice, Michel asked, "Are you all right, Lorne? Would you like to stop?"

"No, I'm fine, just catching my breath." She took a deep breath, which she hoped would calm her racing heart.

"Have we reached the part where your partner was killed?"

"Oh lord, I forgot that part." *How could I forget about Pete like that?* "No, that happened a few days before he held an auction… Oh dear, I'm afraid I'm not doing a very good job at filling in the gaps in your dossier."

"Please go on," he said.

"I don't know if you're aware, but in the Met, we have a unit called CO19. They're an armed response team, the only team in London allowed to carry weapons, which always went against the grain with me." She noticed his brow furrow. "Let me see… I suppose 'annoy' would be the best way of describing that to you."

He nodded, raised a finger of recognition, and then urged her to continue.

"Pete and I received a tip-off of the Unicorn's location, and we were searching an alley when he ambushed us. He was above us, firing from a roof while we were unarmed, so we had no way of retaliating."

"Unarmed, yes, but you were issued with protective vests, *non*?"

"That's a sore point. I had mine done up, but Pete… Well, his didn't fit—he'd put on weight, and his new one hadn't arrived. It meant the fool went in unprotected. Anyway, the Unicorn took Pete out with a bullet to the stomach and another close to the heart. I tried to save him, but…"

"I understand, *chérie*."

His voice and endearment knocked her sideways for a minute or two. It was as though Jacques were in the room with her. Lorne had to dig deep inside herself to continue her story. "No, I don't think you do understand; you couldn't. Pete died in my arms. It's something that will stay with me for the rest of my life. I get flashbacks every waking hour, and I suffer nightmares every night, I can't see that changing any day soon. That image—and hearing the shots that killed Jacques—will torment me forever."

"Maybe I used the wrong word, forgive me. I have never lost a partner."

Lorne dismissed his lack of understanding with a shake of her head. "Not long after that, we discovered that Laura Crane, a member of my team, was feeding information to the Unicorn." Michel gasped. She looked up at him and nodded. "Yes, a mole. That's how he managed to stay ahead of us for so long."

"Why did he involve someone on your team?" Michel surprised her by asking.

"You don't know how many times I've asked myself that same question. I have to admit I've yet to find a suitable answer. Anyway, the Unicorn became more brazen and made contact with me personally—goading me, if you will. He threatened to blow up the Houses of Parliament unless a twenty million–pound ransom was paid. My superintendent refused to take the threat seriously. I had to, though, because the bastard had abducted my daughter."

Michel's face creased with concern. Lorne sucked in a breath. "I'll spare you the details of what he put my thirteen-year-old through—needless to say, she's still seeing a therapist almost a year later. I digress. Due to Charlie—my daughter—being kidnapped, my DCI took over the case until she was returned. He wanted to send me home, but I begged him to let me remain involved. Even my father, an ex-DCI himself, joined us. It's a good job he did, really, as he pointed us in a different direction, urged us to think outside the box. It was then we discovered what the Unicorn was really up to." Lorne watched, slightly amused, as Michel crossed and uncrossed his legs at the ankles continuously with excitement.

"Go on."

"Okay, well, remember I told you the Unicorn or Baldwin was holding the Houses of Parliament to ransom? He gave us a twenty-four hour deadline to meet. To make sure we took his threat seriously, he set off a small incendiary device next door to the proposed target, and as Big Ben struck twelve, my daughter and three other girls were paraded in front of the Houses of Parliament on national TV wearing suicide vests. But that was just the start of our problems. Baldwin went on to kidnap the prime minister's son, shot Charlie and another girl, and the distraction aided his escape."

"What happened next? Did he get away again?"

"I've been talking for too long. To sum it up, he slipped the net and tried to escape on a yacht. The yacht exploded..." Her head dropped as tears misted her vision.

"Forgive me, but how did he escape?"

"By submarine."

"By what?"

"I'm sorry I don't know how else to say it, a boat that travels underwater."

"Yes, yes, sorry. I understand the meaning of the word; I just could not believe it. That must have been some yacht." He let out a long whistle.

"It was worth £250 million."

He whistled again. "You could feed a whole country on that. Sorry, please continue."

"The next day my whole world collapsed—and no, that is not an exaggeration. Pete was buried, my whole family was in hospital—I won't go into detail, there—and then I had to listen to my superintendent and DCI take credit for the case. I resigned, and then Jacques was stolen from me before..." She gazed down at the patterned royal blue carpet as tears cascaded down her cheeks.

Without uttering a word, Michel rose from the bed, covered the short distance between them, and knelt before her. He placed a tentative hand on either side of her face and raised her head to look at him. His thumbs swept across her cheeks, under her eyes, to wipe the tears away. Lorne stared at him, long and hard, looking into his soul through his eyes. Then, she realised what was happening, they were locked in each other's arms, their lips softly parting, inviting each other's tongues to delve into pastures new. His hands stroked her back and sought out every contour of her body. She heard a distant moan of satisfaction and realised the noise had come from her own throat.

Taking her moan as an invitation to continue, Michel swept up her lightweight frame and carried her over to the bed. With their lips still connected, his hands moved swiftly to remove her robe they parted briefly so he could pull the T-shirt over her head, then his lips returned to hers.

As their breaths grew ragged with urgency, Lorne's hands went in search of the buttons on his shirt, but her hands were trembling too much, and her mission became fraught with frustration. Michel took over. Straddling her, he seductively removed his own clothes, tossing them to the floor like old rags.

When they were both finally naked, he gathered her in his arms and whispered. "Let me help the pain disappear, Lorne." She melted into his arms, feeling wanted and desired for the first time in twelve months.

Chapter Thirteen

Something tickled her face. Lorne pulled away and hit her head on the wall. "What the—"

"Shhh, little one. *C'est moi*."

Her cheeks burned when she realised she'd slept with a stranger, but seconds later, she stretched and smiled, feeling relaxed for the first time in months. Michel reached out and gathered her in his arms; she suspected he was looking for a morning encore. His lips touched hers just as someone knocked on the door.

Lorne shot out of bed, feeling like a naughty teenager caught with her first boyfriend in her bedroom. Michel chuckled as he watched her throw on her robe and try to straighten her hair at the same time. "Shut up. Get in there," she ordered, grabbing Michel and shoving him towards the bathroom.

"Just a minute!" she called out as she ran around, picking up their discarded clothes and throwing them in the bathroom after Michel. "Stay there. If I hear one single noise coming from this room, you'll be minced meat, buddy." She started to close the door, but noticed the glint in his eye as he grabbed her arm, to pull her into the room with him.

"*Mais, chérie*. I am not finished with you."

Lorne smiled, then kissed him, hard. "Believe me, Michel, when I tell you I'm far from finished with you, too." She felt a tinge of regret rattle her insides as she wriggled away from him.

The second the door opened, Tony barged past her. "Jeez, Lorne, what kept you?"

"Hey, isn't a lady entitled to some privacy? I was taking a shower. What time is it, anyway?"

One of his eyebrows lifted, "Sure you were, hon. What happened last night? I seem to remember we were about to talk strategies, before you had another 'girly' moment and ran out of the dining room." He glanced aside at the dishevelled bed. "Did we have a restless night?"

She fought hard to stay composed, but her flushing cheeks gave her away. "Every night is restless for me, Tony, as I'm sure you can imagine. I don't wish to appear rude, but couldn't this discussion wait? Over breakfast would be ideal. Give me half an hour, and I'll be down."

A light flickered in his eye. In her eagerness to get rid of him, she'd raised his suspicions. She gulped loudly.

He smiled. "You wouldn't be trying to get rid of me by any chance, Lorne, would you?"

She pulled the robe tight, grabbed him by the arm, and half-tugged, half-pushed him towards the door. "Some guys just can't take a hint. I guess you're one of them, huh, Tony? Now, let me get dressed, will you? In peace."

"All right, all right. No more than half an hour though, Lorne. We'll be on a tight schedule today. How silly of me. I'm sure the *capitaine* has told you that himself already. Isn't that right, *Capitaine*?" he called over his shoulder.

She jettisoned Tony out of the room into the hallway and snapped, "I haven't got the faintest idea what you're going on about."

"Oh, is that right? Well, last night after our meal, the *capitaine* was last seen heading in this direction, and judging by the state of your bed this morning, I'd say he stayed around a little longer than either of you had anticipated." He had pushed her too far and suffered the consequences when she slapped his face. They both froze, but Tony recovered first. "Obviously, my assumption is correct."

Without admitting or denying anything, Lorne felt ashamed and remorseful when she stepped back into the room and closed the door behind her. She stood there, back pressed against the door, her eyes firmly shut.

After a few minutes, a fully clothed Michel came out of the bathroom. "Lorne?" He kissed her on the lips.

"Hmmm…"

He took her in his arms, and she crumpled against his chest as if they'd been lovers for a while rather than just for one night. "Are you upset?"

Lorne pushed herself away from him and gazed into his concerned eyes. "Not really. Let's just say I'm a little confused right now."

"Oh! With us?"

"Honestly?"

"It is the best way."

She laughed despite her topsy-turvy feelings. "I don't know what to think, Michel. About us, about why I'm here, about the direction my life is heading in."

"I understand. I should have been more responsible. I am sorry about what happened last night. Please believe me: It was not my intention to come here to seduce you. It was also not my intention to complicate this case unnecessarily. Do you believe me, Lorne?"

Fresh doubts clawed at her; did that mean he regretted the time they'd spent together? The night of passion neither of them had expected? She nodded, not really knowing what to say.

"Then I must go, let you get dressed. I will see you at breakfast." That time, he didn't finish his sentence with a kiss—a kiss that would have suppressed her fears, given the reassurance her heart was crying out to hear.

Chapter Fourteen

When she walked into the dining room, Lorne found the others deep in conversation, and with butterflies taking flight in her stomach, she sat down in the chair opposite to Michel.

On the table, spread out in front of Michel, were the plans for their intended raid of Baldwin's chateau. He looked up and nodded at her. The smile she'd expected didn't reach his lips or his eyes. *Is that it? You spend the night with me, and all I get as a greeting is a curt nod? Maybe if the lieutenant and Tony hadn't been here, his acknowledgement would have been different.*

"Our teams will be at every exit." Michel informed them with authority.

"How many men?" Tony asked.

"Enough." Michel replied abruptly.

Lorne sensed an atmosphere around the breakfast table that hadn't been there the previous evening at dinner. She couldn't help thinking that what had happened—and what Tony suspected had happened—between the *capitaine* and herself was to blame. Both men were looking at the plan, talking to each other without either using eye contact or each other's names.

"The *gendarmerie* and the national police will be on the scene, as the chateau is located on the border." The *capitaine* looked up to see Lorne raise a quizzical eyebrow. "The national police deal with matters in urban areas, and the *gendarmerie* oversee our rural areas. They have their own swat teams, RAID, GIPN, and GIGN. Usually, these teams work independently, but as we are dealing with such a dangerous man, for the safety of the community, it has been decided that this will be a joint operation."

Lorne nodded, grateful for the explanation, and then asked, "Do we know how many people are inside the chateau?"

"We have heard that Baldwin has many men, at least twenty. All heavily armed and obviously dangerous. The two bodies discovered by fishermen in a nearby lake have been identified as Sergei Osmanov, the Russian Finance Minister, and Chang Foo, the Chinese Finance Minister."

"Do we know why they were here, in France?" Lorne asked.

"We have suspicions, nothing concrete, but for the moment I'd like to keep them close to my chest. Is that the right saying?"

Annoyed that he was trying to keep them out of the loop, Lorne probed further. "If these murders do lead back to the Unicorn—sorry, Baldwin—then what in God's name were two men, both Finance Ministers in their respective governments, doing here? Why come to a sleepy part of France? No disrespect intended, *Capitaine*, but surely these guys are used to holding talks in major cities like London or Paris, not backwaters like this." Her gaze scanned the others before settling on Michel again; she watched as the expression on his face changed several times as her words sunk in.

Finally, after a few minutes' silence, Michel looked up at her, a sparkle in his eyes. "That's very astute of you, Lorne. I can see now why Mr. Warner insisted on bringing you here."

His words knocked her sideways; what had he meant by that? As his words didn't come with a smile attached to them, she couldn't shake the feeling that he'd reprimanded her in some way. "That's as may be, *Capitaine*, but it doesn't tell us why, does it?"

Out the corner of her eye, she caught Tony smirking; she kicked him in the shin.

Michel spotted the smirk, too. "Something amuses you, Mr. Warner?" the *capitaine* asked, through gritted teeth.

"No. Not really."

Michel pushed back his chair. "Very well. I'm drawing this meeting to a close. I suggest we pack our bags and get ready to set off. We will meet again in reception in fifteen minutes." He folded up the plans, tucked them under his arm, and headed out of the dining room.

"So much for going over our strategy," Tony said, expression as surprised as Lorne felt.

When the *lieutenant* followed the *capitaine* out of the room without speaking to either of them, Lorne was left in no doubt that either she or Tony had said—or done—something wrong.

"Idiot!' Lorne tutted.

"What?"

Lorne shook her head. "Maybe it was intentional."

"What was?" Tony asked.

"Him walking out like that. Maybe it's his way of letting us know he's in charge—solely in charge—of the case."

"The man's a bloody idiot, if he thinks that. I ain't gonna put up with that. What about you, Lorne?"

She had an idea where Tony's question was leading. "What about me, Tony?"

"You know. Are you willing to put up with that type of shit from this guy?"

She let out a long sigh. "Grow up, Tony. We're on his patch, for fuck's sake. You know how these things work. His territory, his case, end of."

"It doesn't mean we have to like it, though, does it? The guy comes across as being very cagey. We've had a few meetings with him now, and what information has he given us? Two men have been found murdered close to a chateau belonging to Baldwin—in my book, that doesn't amount to much. There appears to be too much talk and very little action, and it's pissing me off."

She shook her head in frustration. "If you don't agree with how the case is being handled, you know what you can do."

"Sounds to me like you had too much French baguette during the night!"

Lorne expelled another exasperated breath. "I thought we all had the same goal, Tony: to capture Baldwin. We had our chance in England; let's see if the French prove to be better than us, huh? At least give the guy a chance. If you had your way, he would have been sent to the guillotine by now."

"I was just saying—"

"I know what you were *just* saying, Tony, but I'm suggesting that for the sake of civilized Anglo-French relationships, you learn to bite your tongue and put a leash on that temper of yours."

Chapter Fifteen

The chateau, situated in rolling green countryside, was less than twenty minutes from their hotel. Arrangements had been made to meet up with the local police and members of the French SWAT teams at nine that morning. The rendezvous took place half a kilometre from Baldwin's new residence.

The *capitaine*'s car, their car, led the convoy of approximately twenty vehicles, as it meandered its way up the long, narrow, gravelled driveway.

"This looks too easy," Tony whispered out of the corner of his mouth.

Lorne heard his comment but chose to ignore it, more concerned with the hundreds of butterflies that had taken flight in her stomach. She pulled the zipper up on the bullet-proof vest Interpol had provided her for the operation; Tony had already done up his.

The convoy came to a standstill in front of the large oak doors. She and Tony were ordered to stay in the car, they watched as the *capitaine* and the *lieutenant* nonchalantly strolled up to the front door as if they were attending a garden fête.

Tony opened the car door.

"What are you doing?" Lorne asked. "We were told to stay in the car."

"You stay here. I want to see what he says."

"He's French, Tony. You won't be able to understand..." She reached over to try to grab his arm, but he'd already shut the door behind him.

Putting aside the fear churning up her insides, Lorne opened her door and got out. She perched on the bonnet of the car alongside Tony.

"You all right?"

"A bit nervous, I guess. This'll be the first time I've come face-to-face with him," Lorne admitted, her eyes still glued to the front door.

"Hey, relax. My guess is the guy isn't here. Like I said, the drive up here was far too easy. Remember: These guys are notorious for shooting first and asking questions later. It's like a graveyard around here."

The door swung open to reveal a tall, slender man in his late fifties, wearing a traditional butler's outfit. He looked beyond the officers standing at the front door, at the armed entourage, and a look of disbelief registered on his face. As Lorne and Tony eyed the proceedings, they saw the man shrug, then stand aside to let the *capitaine* and *lieutenant* enter the property.

"Too easy!' Tony repeated.

"Let it go, Tony. It'll only fester."

Tony appeared to take umbrage and remained silent for the next ten minutes, until the door to the chateau opened again and the *capitaine* and the *lieutenant* rejoined them.

They were all settled in the car before Tony spoke. "Well?"

"He was not here." Michel stated.

Tony opened his mouth to demand a better answer, but Lorne prodded him painfully in the thigh. He turned and gave her a puzzled look.

"Leave it. Please," she mouthed. He slumped back in his seat, crossed his arms, and stared petulantly in front of him, the way Charlie always did when she didn't get her own way.

The car screeched away, sending the gravel flying in all directions, and they headed back to the hotel.

Lorne couldn't help wondering what would have happened, if all that had taken place on her former patch. Well, for a start, she wouldn't have boldly driven up to the criminal's house and knocked on his front door. Like Tony had suggested, it had all been too easy. *What the hell just happened here? Is Baldwin up to his old tricks, toying with the police again? Did Michel really know what he's up against? If Baldwin wasn't there, where was he?*

Back at the hotel, the *capitaine* instructed the *lieutenant* to make arrangements for them to stay another night.

Lorne grabbed her key and set off towards her room.

Tony was hot on her heels. "What the fuck do you make of that?"

"Now, Tony, calm down."

"Calm down! Don't you dare tell me to calm down, Lorne! Face it, your froggie boyfriend fucked up big time today."

"Right, buster. Let's get a few things straight here: To start with, he's not—I repeat, *not*—my bloody boyfriend. For another, your hands are tied here, Tony; this case is out of your jurisdiction. You knew that when you signed up to help track Baldwin down."

"That's where you're wrong, Lorne. The *capitaine* belongs to Interpol; we are all here as a combined force under the Interpol umbrella."

They reached her room, and Lorne opened the door, Tony followed her in. She dropped down onto her bed and eyed him with suspicion. She could almost see the cogs working in his mind, and she could tell she wasn't going to like what he was about to say. "Okay, big man. Let's have it. I'm guessing you've been planning something during the trip back."

"There's still no flies on you, Lorne, is there? Despite you being out of the field for the past year." He sat down on the bed next to her, and his leg brushed against hers, but she saw through him.

"Stop sucking up and get on with it." She smiled, but her stomach was in knots.

"My suggestion is…we go it alone."

Chapter Sixteen

Lorne sprang to her feet and turned to face him. "I'm sorry, Tony, would you mind repeating that? For a minute there, it sounded like you said something ridiculous like we should contemplate going it *alone*!"

Enouncing every syllable, he repeated, "I did. We go it alone."

"That's what I thought you said. Are you bloody crazy? No, don't answer that, I already know the answer. Shit!" She paced around the room, tracing the full width of it before changing direction and sweeping across the length of it. She came to a halt in front of him. "You've finally gone and lost the plot, man."

Tony laughed long and hard. "Yeah, you're probably right, guilty as charged. But it makes sense, Lorne, you and me as a team. Let's face it, we can't do any worse than the *frogs,* can we?"

"Stop calling him—*them*—that. What makes you think we could do any better?"

"All right, look at it this way. You and I both recognise the operation today was downright farcical. If that had been an English operation, there's no way we would've considered turning up at the chateau like that. I know, I know—we don't have chateaus in England," he said, as she opened her mouth to correct him. "His reputation alone would make us ultra-cautious. He's a murdering bastard through and through, for fuck's sake. These guys approached that chateau as if they were on a coppers' day out, a picnic in the country or something equally as banal. Come on, admit it: You were as frustrated as I was." He tilted his head and waited for her to respond.

She waved her hands in the air. "All right, Tony, yes. I admit I was as frustrated as you, but I still don't see what options we have. What can we possibly do about it? Bottom line is we'd be foolish to even consider it. Baldwin's armed, probably to the hilt, and Michel has already informed us that Baldwin has at least twenty men with him patrolling the chateau." She plonked herself down on the bed beside him.

"And that's another thing. Where was Baldwin today? More to

the point, where were all his men? The useless *frog* didn't even search the place, for Christ's sake."

"He went inside the building."

"Yeah, for ten whole minutes. What the blazes could he check in that amount of time? And, how come he and the *lieutenant* were the only ones to step foot inside the joint?"

"What are you getting at now?"

With a note of sarcasm Tony retorted, "Now, let's see. We trundle up to the chateau—in broad daylight, I hasten to add—only to find Baldwin long gone. Mere coincidence? I doubt it. All we have to figure out is who the possible mole is, the *capitaine*—your secret lover—or the *lieutenant*."

"I'm going to let that one pass, Tony, and I'm warning you if I hear another wisecrack about Michel and myself, then I'm on the first plane out of here. Do you hear me?" She prodded him in the chest.

"Ouch! Whatever, Lorne, but even you can't deny there's something dodgy going on here. Look at what happened back in England, that Lorna girl on your team. Tell me I'm wrong."

"Yeah, you're wrong. It was Laura, not Lorna."

"Whatever her bloody name was, she still did the business, didn't she? Disrupted your investigation and told Baldwin precisely what was going on—"

"And got herself killed into the bargain."

"Comeuppance, that's what that's called, Lorne. Just desserts. She played with fire far longer than she should have, and she got burned in the end."

"All right, there's no need for you to keep going over old ground. What *plan* have you come up with? What's up your sleeve, agent boy?"

"How do I know I can trust you? What assurances can you give me that you won't divulge anything during your secret assignations with the *capitaine*?"

She spotted a smile in his eyes, and she had an inkling he was just winding her up, so she thumped him hard—hard enough to give him a dead leg. "Just so you know, Tony, that was a one-off. It's not something I intend repeating. Now, give! My curiosity is piqued."

Instead of telling her his plans as she'd expected, Tony rose from the bed and headed for the door.

"Hey, wait up, agent boy!"

He tapped his nose, opened the door, and stepped into the hallway, turning to wink at her. "Leave everything to me. All you have to do is keep the *capitaine* entertained for the next few hours— and I'm sure you don't need me to draw you any diagrams on how you can manage that, now do you, Lorne?"

Chapter Seventeen

The cheeky little shit. What the hell did he take me for, some kind of prostitute? Lorne tried to come up with a suitable plan to keep Michel occupied for the next few hours, but apart from jumping on his bones like a sex-starved virgin, she couldn't think what to say or do without giving the game away.

A knock at the door disturbed her thoughts, which were dwelling on a plan that included sex.

Christ, this place is busier than Oxford Street during the January sales!

She ran into the bathroom to check her appearance in the mirror, then returned to open the door. "Oh, *Capitaine*! I wasn't expecting you." Her words came out in a husky breath, which annoyed her.

Michel was leaning his head against the doorframe, his face expressionless, making it difficult for her to read, though she did spot a certain glint in his eye that both excited and unnerved her at the same time.

Is he waiting for me to invite him in? Is it possible he wants to pick up where we left off last night?

Appearing to read her mind, he asked, "Do you intend to ask me in, or do you want to have a conversation out here? Actually, on second thought, let's go out. There is little we can do here anyway, except twiddle our thumbs. Forgive me—is that the right expression?"

"As usual, Michel, you're spot on with your meaning, but where will we go?" Lorne asked, relieved that she wouldn't need to fall back on her womanly charms to distract him, like Tony had so vulgarly suggested. An outing with him would get him out of the way just fine, and if he was on Baldwin's payroll, she doubted he would try anything while Tony was around.

"Do I need to change?" She queried, looking down at what she was wearing: jeans, T-shirt, jumper.

"No. The clothes you wear will be suitable."

Michel drove. They left the hotel at close to midday, the September sun bathing them in warmth. The surprise trip took them approximately half an hour by car, the quiet journey more contented than awkward, like last time.

Michel dropped down a gear as the winding road grew busier, and it wasn't long before they came to a halt, a long queue of cars in front of them, stretching as far as the eye could see.

"Can I ask where we're going?" she asked.

"You can ask, yes. Whether I reply or not is another matter." Michel laughed.

Suddenly, the inside of the car felt hot and stuffy. Lorne pushed the button on the armrest next to her elbow to open the car window a fraction. She glanced sideways at him and thought she'd spotted a calmness seeping into his features that she'd not seen before. Sensing their journey would soon come to an end, she pushed back into the headrest, forcing herself to relax.

Minutes later, they pulled into a half-full car park. To the right stood at least a dozen coaches. The drivers stood in a group outside their vehicles, waiting for their passengers to return. They seemed to be enjoying their sandwiches and cans of soda, taking the opportunity to bathe in the sun's rays.

Lorne's mouth dropped open at the sight of half a dozen American Jeeps, all shiny and beautifully presented, parked beneath a large sign by the entrance that read, 'Colleville-Sur-Mer American war cemetery'. *What a funny place to bring a date. Why here?*

"You seem confused by my choice. I assure you, you will not be disappointed. I used to come here often as a child. Once you have visited this place, your outlook on life will be changed forever— whether that change will be for the better, only you can decide. Come on."

He was right. She did feel confused and also perplexed by his words. *What did he mean, "Your outlook on life will be changed forever"?*

After he locked the car, Michel took her hand in his, surprising her, and he led her through the beautifully tended gardens and past the visitor centre. Situated on the cliff-face high above the sea, the cemetery was a magnificent sight.

They entered through a large metal gate. Before them stood a semi-circular wall constructed of white marble, measuring, she guessed, around three hundred feet in length. The sweet smell of roses in full bloom welcomed them like a long-lost relative with open arms. Although sixty or so people filled the area, only the rustling of the trees above could be heard. People young and old moved slowly around the wall, reading the text etched into the stone.

"Oh my God," she whispered, as it dawned on her what the writing said.

Michel bent to whisper in her ear, "This is the 'garden of the missing'. Some 1557 servicemen are listed here. Their remains have never been found."

Lorne lifted her head to look at him, and unexpected tears welled up in her eyes. He comforted her by putting his arm around her shoulder and pulling her close. She sensed he had a good idea what she was going through, and the people she was thinking about. She rested her head on his chest and together, side-by-side, they silently continued on their bewildering journey, both deep in thought.

They climbed the stone steps that divided the wall, and Michel's grip tightened, as if he was preparing for her to be shocked. Before them, laid out in symmetrical rows, stood thousands of white crosses. Every now and then a Star of David broke up the immaculate lines.

"Good lord!" Lorne said, coming to a halt at the top of the steps.

"Truly remarkable, *non*?"

"And some," Lorne replied. They were now standing in the centre of the colonnaded memorial. On either side of them lay maps, engraved in stone, accompanied by text that documented the progress of the Allied forces on the D-day beaches of Normandy. As the crowds gathered around them, Michel took Lorne by the elbow and led her past the huge reflecting pool, towards the tiny circular chapel located a few hundred feet beyond. Inside, Lorne let out a loud gasp when she gazed up at the colourful fresco ceiling that detailed every aspect of the war.

Once they stepped back outside of the chapel, Michel acted like a tour guide, and informed Lorne of relevant facts and figures about the cemetery. As they moved through the gravestones and headed towards the cliff, he said, "To the left is Omaha beach. Today it is beautiful, sandy, and serene—but back in 1944, the golden sands were soaked in blood. A chaotic area filled with death and casualties."

His hand swept over the area behind them. "It is where the majority of these men died. The Germans were lying in wait for them to come ashore. These men died saving *our* country, and making sure the rest of Europe did not fall into Hitler's despicable hands. There are 9387 graves situated here. This is the first American cemetery on European soil. It stands in 172 acres. You see the statue over there?" He pointed to a bronze statue at least thirty feet tall, standing on a pedestal.

She nodded, awestruck by the amount of detail he knew about the cemetery.

"It is called the 'Spirit of American Youth'." He paused to swallow before telling her more. "The average age of those who died and who are buried here is just twenty-two."

"My God. How awful."

"Have you seen the film *Saving Private Ryan?*" She nodded again. "Two of the Ryan brothers are buried here—different name, of course. That was fiction. In 2004, the sixtieth anniversary of D-day, Tom Hanks and Steven Spielberg personally attended the commemoration ceremony held here."

"I remember. At the back of my mind, I seem to recall seeing a clip that was shown on news at ten. That sounds awful, doesn't it?"

"What do you mean?" Michel raised an eyebrow.

"Something so historical, that I should pass it off with a statement like 'somewhere in the back of my mind'. Look around you, Michel. Without the goodwill of these unselfish men, sacrificing their precious lives, you have to ask the question: what, where, or how would we be living today?" Lorne felt humbled by her surroundings.

"I'm sorry." Michel placed a gentle arm under her elbow and guided her towards the exit and his car.

"Sorry for what?"

"For bringing you here. It can be overwhelming for some people, even gloomy in some respects."

She stopped halfway across the car park and looked up at him. "That's nonsense, Michel. I'm pleased you thought to share this place with me. How can you think otherwise?"

"Your own situation. I did not think. Forgive me, Lorne, for unintentionally opening up recent painful wounds."

She shook her head slowly. "Michel, believe it or not, coming here has helped put my own pitiful life into perspective. I've wallowed in my own self-pity far too long. I will always treasure the time I spent with Pete and Jacques, but after visiting here today, it has made me realise how short life really is. No matter how much we hurt when loved ones pass, our lives must go on. No matter what

He—or anybody else—cares to throw at us." She raised her eyes to the hazy blue sky that was dotted with the odd white fluffy cloud.

Michel kissed her gently on the cheek but said nothing as he opened the car door for her.

"Where to now?" She felt free all of a sudden, free from the weight that had been weighing her down for the past year—free to continue her life, to live each day fully, without pain or regret. As though somehow, back in the cemetery, she'd set Pete's and Jacques' spirits free.

"It's a ten-minute journey to Omaha beach, if you would like to see it?"

"I'd love to." She settled her head back in the seat and closed her eyes.

Chapter Eighteen

For the next few hours, Lorne and Michel strolled hand in hand along the wide expanse of fine, sandy beach. Omaha beach had proved to be just as thought-provoking as the cemetery, and they walked in silence, the only sound the gentle one of the waves breaking on the edge of the beach.

They arrived back at the hotel sometime after six, and following a quick shower and change of clothes in their respective rooms, they joined the others in the dining room at seven thirty.

Dinner consisted of salmon fillet, served in a white wine sauce, with green beans and dauphinois potatoes, followed by a chocolate and pear tart, which was accompanied by a scoop of vanilla ice cream—all of which Lorne managed to select for herself. Working out that *saumon* was *salmon* didn't tax her too much, and she was sure that anything chocolate was bound to taste good even to her unadventurous palate.

Lorne spotted the suspicion on the faces of both Tony and the *lieutenant* as she joined them at the table, though they said nothing. The conversation was light-hearted, touching on exactly why the French called the English 'Les Rosbifs'—'roast beef'—and turning to the differences in English and French police procedures. Tony, however, ended the evening with bruised shins as Lorne sought to keep him from launching into areas that might embarrass their French hosts. He was easy to read; Lorne had noticed he shifted in his seat whenever he was about to stray into difficult territory, and a swift kick to the shins brought him back into line.

When the dinner ended at ten o'clock, Lorne bade good night to the others, feeling worn out both emotionally and physically, and headed for her room, alone. She doubted very much if her emotions could have withstood another night in the arms of Michel Amore.

By the time she had removed her makeup, cleaned her teeth, and dressed for bed, it was already a quarter to eleven. She drifted off to sleep almost immediately, but her dreams were filled with men dying, their blood seeping into the sand of Omaha beach. The sound of distant machine gunfire proved too much for her, and she woke with a jolt.

Lorne turned on the bedside light and mopped her sweating brow with a tissue from the box beside her bed. The dream had felt so real, the gunfire—there it was again

She realised it was someone knocking on her door.

She looked at her alarm clock. *What the heck? Nearly two in the morning.* She grabbed her robe and pulled open the door, her face screwed up in anger when she saw who was standing on the other side.

Tony barged straight past her. "Glad to see you're alone."

"What the hell do you want?" Lorne asked, matching his offhand tone.

"Get dressed," her uninvited guest ordered.

"What? Are you crazy? It's the bloody middle of the night, Tony!"

"Einstein strikes another home run. Get dressed, Lorne. Now."

"Not until you tell me what in God's name is going on here." She folded her arms and tapped her foot.

"And they say men are the more stubborn of the two genders. I've got a hired car waiting outside. Now get your pretty arse into gear, will you?"

"Where are we going at such a late hour?"

His hand swept through his hair as his patience rocked and rolled. "The bloody chateau. We're going on a reconnaissance trip of our own. Now will you get dressed, *please*?"

Without further argument, Lorne gathered clean underwear and the final clean outfit she'd brought with her—which just happened to be black jeans and a black sweater, ideal getup for a night-time prowler—and disappeared into the bathroom.

She reappeared five minutes later, dressed and feeling apprehensive about the adventure she knew lay ahead of them.

Chapter Nineteen

"You're going the wrong way." Lorne turned in the passenger seat and pointed behind her. "It was that road back there, I'm sure of it."

He patted her thigh and laughed. "That's why men don't ask women to navigate that often. They tend to have a lousy sense of direction." The road they were searching for materialized in front of them. "I rest my case—oh, and apology accepted."

Her face screwed up in anger, she aimed a fist at his arm and mumbled, "You smug bag of shit."

"Ouch, what the hell was that for?"

"Wuss! Has anyone ever told you how infuriating you can be at times, agent boy?"

"Kinda lost count of how many people have told me that. I'll add your name to the list, shall I?"

She didn't bother responding.

In front of them, the outline of the chateau came into view. Her stomach churned, and it felt like the knots had begun to constrict her intestines. Even at night, with the moon dipped behind a low cloud, the place had an air of grandeur. A strange thought popped into her head: *I wonder if this chateau has ever been used as a film set.*

Jesus, what the hell are we doing here? Why in God's name did I let Tony talk me into this? I don't know who's crazier: him, for suggesting this adventure, or me, for agreeing to come!

Another thing that unsettled her was the fact that they hadn't told anyone about their mission. *If anything goes wrong... No, nothing will go wrong because Tony is an expert in his field.*

"You do know what you're doing, Tony, don't you?"

"You worry too much, trust me. And why are you whispering?"

Now she really was worried; the last person who'd told her to trust him had been Pete. Not long after, she'd been standing in a church, reciting a eulogy at his funeral.

Tony went on to reassure her. "Lorne, I mean it—trust me, will you? If I had any doubts or thought there would be any trouble, I would've gone it alone. You'd be back at the hotel, nice and cosy, tucked up in your warm bed." He squeezed the top of her thigh, turned off the lights, and changed down a gear. They crawled along the gravelled driveway and came to halt halfway down, behind an eight-foot yew hedge.

"How will we get in?" Lorne whispered again.

Tony reached into the inside pocket of his black jacket and pulled out a carefully folded sheet of paper, which he spread across the steering wheel in front of him before taking out a small flashlight from another pocket.

Her eyes widened. "Where the hell did you get that?"

"While you were out with the *capitaine*, I had a little snoop in his room."

"You mean you *stole* them? Jesus, Tony. What if he discovers they're missing? Have you thought about that? About the implications of what you've done?"

"I'm going to say this only once, Lorne, and the choice is yours: If you want to back out and stay in the car, then by all means do it. But I'm going in."

"What about the men? We don't know if they have dogs guarding the place."

"When we came this morning, I observed their security measures, and basically, there aren't any. No dogs, anyway. Mind you, his men are probably all the guard dogs he needs."

He gave her a brief smile before returning his attention to the plans. "All the windows are small, except these ones here." He pointed to a few situated at the rear, on the ground floor. "Are you in or out, hon?"

Lorne silently surveyed the huge chateau. She sensed Tony getting agitated beside her.

Finally, he folded up the plan, reached for the handle and threw open the car door. "In or out?" he asked over his shoulder. Lorne pushed open her own door and climbed out of the vehicle in response. "Good girl."

They ducked down. To avoid the crunch of the gravel beneath their feet, they ran along the damp grass on the edge of the driveway, making for the rear of the property. They stopped outside the window Tony had highlighted on the plan. He pulled out a small black case from another of his inside pockets. "Tools of the trade." Unzipping the case, he extracted a pointed instrument approximately six inches in length.

Standing at full height, he secured one end of the tool to the glass with the attached suction cap and held it there with the heel of his hand, while he used the other end to cut a full circle. A high-pitched scraping noise accompanied the movement, but it only took a few seconds to complete the job. Tony removed the circle, placing it on the ground beside Lorne. He reached through the hole, pulled up the handle, and the window opened inwards. "*Et voilà.*"

Tony hoisted himself up onto the ledge and stuck his head in. Satisfied no one was around, he hopped back down. "It seems to be clear. Come on, I'll give you a bunk up."

Lorne placed her foot in his flattened hand, and as she jumped, he placed his other hand on her backside to steady her. "Oi, you!" She just managed to slap his hand away before she tumbled through the opening. She landed with a thump on the cold concrete floor. After a quick brush down, she pulled herself flat against the stone wall to wait for Tony.

He came through the window, himself. "That's the easy part done."

The smell of spices filled the air of the pantry, making her nose twitch. *Don't you dare sneeze.*

They reached an old gnarled oak door, Tony turned the circular black cast iron handle, but the door refused to budge. "Shit! It's locked."

He crouched down and peered through the keyhole. "That's a blessing. The key's not there." Out popped his bag of tricks again, and he positioned yet another tool in the hole, wiggled it about until she heard a subtle click. Looking over his shoulder, he gloated, "I'm just too good for words."

She dug the egotist in the ribs, shuddered, and whispered urgently, "Just get on with it, Tony. Get what you need, and let's get the hell out of here. I've got a bad feeling about this!"

Tony's pen-torch lit their path and guided them through the property, their footsteps a distant slap on the cold concrete slabs in the hallway. With Tony leading the way and Lorne holding onto the tail of his jacket, they made their way down the hallway and then through the door into one of the rooms on the ground floor. He switched on the light switch.

"What the hell are you doing?"

"Calm down. Stop hyperventilating, woman. It's quite safe. I checked there were no windows in here, first. Right, what have we got here?" He walked towards the monitors lining one of the walls.

"This appears to be his eyes to the outside world. His security den, his Operations room, if you like."

"Shit!' She pointed at the far monitor. Their car, which Tony had thought would be well screened, was clearly visible, thanks to the camera's obscure angle. "He'll know we've been here."

"Easily sorted, Lorne. We'll take the relevant security tape with us when we leave," the levelheaded agent reassured her. His inspection of the equipment soon revealed it didn't run on tapes, instead using state-of-the-art surveillance that fed all the camera footage to a hard drive, instead of tapes or discs.

Tony saw a bottle of water on the table and poured it into the front of the computer tower. "That should take care of that." He studied the monitors and picked out two possible rooms they should check out. "That's where we should be heading: Baldwin's bedroom and his office."

"Any idea where we're going to find them?" she asked, her gaze flitting around the screens, constantly on the lookout for any kind of movement.

Tony anticipated her question and had the plan ready. "It doesn't state which room is which on here, but I think we can safely assume this one is Baldwin's bedroom; it's the room with the most square footage and is the only one with an en-suite. We'll head for that one—shit, it *would* be located at the far end of the corridor. I can't tell where the office is, though; it'll be a case of popping our heads into each room until we hit the jackpot."

"That's ridiculous, Tony. You're forgetting something." Her voice came out higher than normal, betraying that her nerves had started to jangle.

"What's that?"

"The butler. He's got to be in here somewhere. Look on the plan again. Does anything say 'servants' quarters' or anything similar to that?"

Tony scanned the plan. He tapped a smaller room at the top of the staircase and turned to her. "This could be his room—I say *could* be. To be honest, I'd forgotten all about him. We'll have to be extra cautious, mind you. The guy looked harmless enough, but who's to say what weapons he might have hidden under his bed?"

"Thanks for that. Just what a girl wants to hear. I feel at ease now, agent boy—*not.*"

Tony shrugged an apology. "Come on. Let's get a move on." He switched the light off as Lorne grabbed the tail of his jacket again and followed him out into the dark hallway.

He moved swiftly, and Lorne admired the way he expertly guided both of them through the hallway and up the stone stairway. A thrill crept up her spine as it dawned on her she'd never entered a criminal's house before without a search warrant in her hand.

She shuddered when yet another strange thought struck her: They were trespassing. She wondered if Tony loved his job so much because of the thrill factor involved. A year ago, when she had resigned from the force, he had tried to recruit her. She'd turned him down, thinking the job wasn't really for her, but now…

Tony stopped. Lorne, still deep in thought, piled into the back of him.

"Shh!" he scolded. "Do you want to wake up the butler, you idiot?"

"Sorry."

They tiptoed past the room they presumed to be the butler's quarters and set off down the long narrow corridor, the tiny flashlight still guiding their way. Tony halted outside a door on his left and ordered her to poke her head round the door on the opposite side of the hallway. Nothing. Their search went on.

The same routine took place at the next set of rooms and again their exploration proved to be fruitless. Their luck changed, however, when Tony tried the next door on his side, and they entered the room.

"What are we supposed to be looking for, Tony?" she whispered, squinting into the darkness of the room.

He shrugged, then whispered, "Fucked if I know."

His words made her pause and look at him, her mouth open in disbelief. "You're kidding me! Some kind of clue would be helpful."

"If I knew what I was bloody looking for, I would have come alone. I wouldn't have involved you. I brought you along to make use of your detecting skills. So get cracking, if anything looks out of place, give me a shout."

"Great. Truly helpful, agent boy."

"Lorne."

"Yeah?"

"Will you for Christ's sake stop calling me 'agent boy'? I'm thirty-eight years old, in case you hadn't noticed."

She pulled a face at him, then riffled through the papers on the mahogany leather-inlaid desk. Tony handed her a spare flashlight, and she waded through paper after paper. They were mainly in French, so she had to guess, but she was fairly sure they were utility bills. "Nothing, just the usual crap paperwork," she complained.

"Stop moaning, Lorne. Look in the filing cabinet over there." She looked over her shoulder and headed for the green cabinet. Before she opened it, he warned, "Make sure you open the drawers quietly."

She scowled and gave him the finger. "I might be a bit rusty, agent boy, but I haven't lost my intelligence altogether, thanks."

He cringed, tutted, and shook his head.

Lorne heard Tony open the unlocked drawers in the desk. "Bingo," he whispered.

She turned to see him taking photos of an open file with his mobile.

"What's that?" she asked, crossing the room to stand alongside him.

"If it's what I think it is, these details should match up to Interpol's stolen art database, making it our ticket out of here. I'll just take some pictures, then we'll be off."

The word *paintings* was written on the file's tab, and the sheets Tony had been photographing contained a list of numbers and names.

Through the corner of her eye, she saw something flicker and moved over to the window. "Shit! We've got company." Her eyes remained fixed on the car headlights heading up the drive towards them.

"Fuck, the butler was probably out all along. Two more minutes, then I'm done."

Lorne watched and swallowed down the bile rising in her throat. Her heart thumped faster as the car slowly drove up the drive. *How the hell did I get myself in this mess? What if that's Baldwin coming back? What if it's not the butler returning home, after all?* So many questions and so few answers.

Tony's camera continued to click away at the file. "For Pete's sake, Tony." She winced at her choice of words. *Sorry, mate. Feel free to lend a hand, though!*

"Okay, okay. That's it." He slammed the file shut and returned it to the drawer. They both froze and looked at each other, eyes wide and fearful as the ominous sound of crunching gravel drifted up from the courtyard below.

Chapter Twenty

"What the fuck do we do, now?" Lorne asked.

Tony had joined her at the window, and they watched a tall thin figure step out of the vehicle and approach the front of the chateau.

"We wait."

"For what, exactly?"

He let out a heavy sigh, glared at her, and placed a finger to his lips. The front door slammed shut. Tony pointed at the desk and ordered her to get under it. He wedged himself in beside her.

"What happens now?" Lorne asked, her back already beginning to ache in the cramped space.

"And I wonder why I prefer to work alone," he mumbled, tilting his head to listen. They both heard movements coming from the kitchen below. Lorne let his sarcasm slip by.

Twenty minutes later, the cramp in her legs—likely his, too—felt unbearable. They heard heavy footfalls on the stairs. Lorne listened, her heart furiously pounding, when a door closed further down the hallway. Still, neither of them dared to move.

Tony whispered, "Give it half an hour, then we'll make a move, all right?"

"My legs won't hold out that long," she whined, tears of frustration springing to her eyes.

"Okay, ten more minutes. It should be safe to get out from under here then, but we'll have to stay in the room for another twenty minutes. That way your legs will have a chance to regain some feeling."

She nodded and tried to relax her muscles.

"See, I'm not a bastard all the time. I do take time off, occasionally." He smiled, then surprised her by rubbing his hands vigorously up and down her legs to help improve her circulation.

Thirty minutes later, Tony poked his head into the hallway. He grabbed Lorne's hand, and they pressed their backs against the wall and eased their way down the hallway again.

It seemed an eternity before they reached the bottom step. They retraced their steps through the house.

When they reached the car, a tear of relief slipped down Lorne's cheek.

Tony shook his head. "Not again, woman."

"*What?*" She shouted tetchily, not caring if she was heard by anyone in the chateau.

"Christ, the amount of tears you've cried lately, I'm surprised you're not permanently dehydrated."

She suspected he was joking, but she felt raw. She gave him the finger and a solid glare before she wiped the tear away with her sleeve.

They arrived back at the hotel at almost four in the morning to the amusement of the night porter, and they hopped into the lift feeling embarrassed. "I hope discretion was on the agenda of his night porter courses," Tony said.

Lorne felt drained, her muscles tight from the tension thrown at them during their dangerous assignment. All she wanted to do was to curl up in her nice warm bed and catch up on some sleep.

The lift pinged when it reached their floor, and the doors slid open to reveal Capitaine Michel Amore: his arms folded firmly across his chest, his face set like stone, and his foot tapping. "And where the hell have you two been?"

Chapter Twenty-One

Tony spoke first. "Would you believe us if we said we just popped out for a midnight stroll?"

"Impossible. By my watch, it is past four. I will ask my question one more time—and this time, Lorne, *you* will give me an honest answer. Where have you been?"

God, what is it with these men? Why do they think us women will simply roll over and tell all? Her cheeks warm, she focused on a gold swirl in the patterned blue carpet, just in front of Michel's feet. The lift doors *whooshed* several times, but Tony's large foot prevented them from closing. An uncomfortable silence surrounded them; all that could be heard was the sound of heavy breathing.

Clearly angered, Michel sucked in his cheeks, making his eyes appear to double in size. After ordering them out of the lift, he turned his back and marched up the corridor towards his room, expecting Lorne and Tony to fall into step behind him. A shiver of trepidation rippled through her tired body.

Tony leaned over and whispered, "You all right?"

Her eyes fluttered shut for the briefest of seconds, and when she reopened them, she gave him a look that said, "This is another fine mess you've gotten me tangled up in."

They entered the lion's den, and Michel shut the door behind them. "Take a seat," Michel ordered.

The pair sat on his messed-up bed. *So he had been to bed, then. How and when did he realise we were missing? Did he knock on my door, hoping for an encore, and discover me gone?*

Michel's angry voice broke into her reverie, "As you have refused to answer me, I will tell you where I believe you were tonight. Before I do, I must warn you—do not take me for an incompetent *foreign* fool. Do I make myself clear?"

Lorne remained silent, her downcast eyes focusing on the *capitaine*'s shoes. She cringed when Tony pretended to clear his throat, obviously finding the Frenchman's threat-slash-warning amusing.

Before she had the chance to look at Tony, Michel had crossed the divide between them quicker than a hare out of the traps at a greyhound meeting. Grabbing Tony's shirtfront and collar, he yanked him to his feet. Lorne gasped and watched in disbelief as the hatred rippled back and forth between the two men.

Jumping up, Lorne ducked under the *capitaine*'s outstretched arms and squeezed her five-foot-five inches between them. "Come on, guys. We're supposed to be on the same team here."

Michel shoved Tony away. He looked down at Lorne with narrowed eyes. "That's what I thought too, Madame Simpkins."

"Hey, don't lay the blame at Lorne's door, buster."

"Oh, I assure you, Mr. Warner, I hold you *both* responsible for disobeying... No, that is the wrong word." He thought for a moment. "No, *violating*, would be a more suitable word to sum up your actions tonight. You have *violated* both mine and my country's trust. That is something I will not tolerate. At first light, I will arrange for you to be escorted to the airport and sent back to England. Your country might put up with such dishonourable actions, but I am afraid in France, we pride ourselves to solve cases by the book."

"Probably makes sense why Baldwin has settled here, then. He views France as an easy touch," Tony said.

"Why, you—"

The *capitaine* charged at Tony, but again Lorne jumped between the two pig-headed men. "Cut it out! This isn't going to solve anything."

She had a hand on each of their tensed chests, her head swivelling between them as they glared and snarled at each other, neither man willing to back down. It wasn't long before her wrists ached from the pressure of trying to keep them apart. Finally, she snapped, jumping in the air she landed on both of the men's feet. "Jesus, guys... Give it a rest, will you? No wonder Baldwin runs rings around the police. You two are acting like a few bloody Keystone Cops." Sapped of strength, she collapsed backwards onto the bed.

"I think you should take back your accusation, Mr. Warner." Michel rubbed his sore foot up and down the calf of his other leg.

Lorne lifted her gaze to the ceiling. *Jesus, these two could start their own world war right in this very room.*

"That's impossible, *Capitaine*. In England, Baldwin never settled anywhere. Lorne will vouch for me on that score, won't you, Lorne?"

Big mouth. Keep me out of your petty squabbles, will you? I'm retired from the force, remember!

The way both men turned to look at her, she sensed each man expected her to come down on his side. She nodded, not wanting to be in an invidious position, and shrugged.

"Your logic is unfathomable at times, Mr. Warner. Maybe…Mr. Baldwin did not care for your country. Perhaps, he prefers to live here," Michel said.

"Bullshit! That's bollocks, in any language. He knows how gullible you French are. He's aware how *grateful* the French can be when someone throws a few million around. Regardless of the fact his entire fortune happens to be illegally obtained."

The tension intensified, and Lorne physically jumped when the phone by the bed rang.

Michel answered it. "*Oui, daccord. Je compris, je regret.*" He slammed down the receiver. "That was reception. The people in the rooms either side have complained. They asked us to keep the noise down. I suggest we resume our *discussion* in the morning. Maybe our heads will be clearer and cooler by then."

He glanced at his watch. "We will rendezvous in three hours." He marched over to the door and threw it open, giving them little option but to comply.

Tony stormed out and headed down the hallway towards his own room. Lorne hesitated in the doorway and looked deep into Michel's eyes, silently pleading with him to forgive her disloyalty. Without saying a word, he grabbed her shoulders. Expecting him to take her in his arms, Lorne expelled a relieved breath. Instead, Michel spun her towards the door, moved one of his hands to the centre of her back, and nudged her over the threshold.

Dumbfounded and hoping to plead her case further, Lorne turned to face him, only to find the door shut and juddering in its frame. She stared at it, stinging from the insult and wondering if it was hatred she'd seen in Michel's eyes, the same eyes that, barely twenty-four hours before, had emanated sincerity during their lovemaking.

She shuddered as she struggled to deal with the hurt steadily rising. Her shoulders slumped in defeat, and she headed back to her room, alone.

Jesus, Lorne. There's just no stopping you at times, is there, girl? "Mrs. Mess-up"—the blunders just keep on coming, don't they? And sleeping with Michel has to be right up there with the best of them.

She cursed her own weakness, jumped into bed, and buried her head under the quilt, in shame.

Chapter Twenty-Two

After receiving the tip-off that the police were about to raid the chateau, Baldwin had ordered Julio to get his private jet ready for a trip and given his men some time off, instructing them to report back for duty in forty-eight hours. The jet had landed in Monaco a few hours later around mid-afternoon. With some R&R on the agenda, the two men boarded Baldwin's £350 million yacht, the yacht he'd cheated a Sheikh in Dubai out of, in a dodgy game of poker.

The 525-foot yacht, with its four diesel engines and 9,000 horse power, had dropped anchor just outside the harbour walls of France's notorious millionaires' playground, bobbing away peacefully on the slight swell of the Mediterranean. A few smaller yachts, less than half the size of *Lady Luck*, were dotted around them, anchored a few hundred feet apart, following the unspoken rule for sailors to respect others' privacy.

"Ah, this is the life, Julio, huh? Sun, sea, and sex on tap. Not a care in the world. Millions of pounds, dollars, euros, and yen dripping into my account. Three more weeks, and the title will be mine: 'the world's richest man'." He laughed, a jovial belly laugh.

The rest of the group joined him, including the two large-breasted blonde bimbo-looking *mesdemoiselles*, despite not understanding a word of what the rich Englishman was saying. But Baldwin expected that. When he'd sent Julio ashore to pick up a few girls, his instructions had been clear. He wanted the three *B*'s: breasts, beauty, and brainless. The girls had been cherry-picked, with the aid of Julio flashing his bulging wallet around, and the two selected were undeniably lacking in the IQ and conversational skills departments. As an added bonus, the two girls were 'first-timer' prostitutes.

Julio slapped the backside of the blonde who was curled up on his lap, dozing in the sun. *Chambre numéro deux*," he said, trying out his schoolboy French.

The girl giggled, wriggled off his lap, slipped on a pair of deck shoes, and wrapped her bikini-clad body in a towelling robe.

Smiling, Julio shook his head, ripped the robe off the girl, and threw it overboard. "You won't be needing that." He spun the girl around, patted her cute little arse, and pointed to the stairs leading down to one of the five VIP suites. They went below. The sound of slapped flesh and giggles followed the randy pair, until the noise of a door being slammed shut drifted up to the deck.

The other girl sat on the end of Baldwin's wooden steamer, giving him a fake bashful smile. He grabbed her hair. Picking up the end of one of her pigtails, he sucked on it, then smiled at her invitingly, before licking his lips and beckoning her with his finger. Using her breasts as if they were her hands, she teased her way up the length of his body, stroking his shins, then his thighs. It didn't take long for his penis to double in size.

Tugging at the strings on either side of her bikini bottoms, he released the tiny piece of aqua blue material, and it fluttered to the deck. His eyes dropped to his Speedos then back up to her pretty freckled face. She grasped his meaning immediately. He lifted his backside off the lounger, and she tugged down his trunks. The girl tried to kiss him on the lips, but he turned his face to the side. Taken aback, the French girl frowned and looked hurt, but Baldwin wasn't the type to let someone's hurt feelings bother him.

Again, using only his eyes to communicate, Baldwin glanced down at his cock, then back up at the girl. He watched a light bulb of comprehension register in the bimbo's brain.

She placed her warm, wet lips around his penis. He groaned as his hands sought out the pigtails on either side of her head. Yanking on them, he pulled her head down at the same time as he thrust his hips upwards—faster and faster, making the girl gag, but he ignored her flailing arms and the way her lips pushed against his penis, trying to force the offending item out of her mouth.

Eventually, he shot his load. Feeling exhausted from his exertions, he rested his head back against the cushion. Meanwhile, the girl seized the opportunity to escape. She scrabbled around under the steamer, looking for her bikini. The sound of her sobbing as she covered herself with the flimsy garment pissed him off. He'd experienced sluts all his life, and when things started to get rough, the whining usually began, and his patience snapped.

He sneered at the girl, watched her shudder. A malevolent fascination tinged with a spark of excitement filled him. Hairs on the back of his neck stood to attention. A half-smile curled his lips. He patted the steamer beside him, inviting the girl to sit down.

She hesitated, but when his lips pulled into a full smile, he saw her defences weaken. Slowly, she sat on the end of the steamer and moved cautiously towards him, her movements filled with trepidation and fear. Then, before she had a chance to stop him, he tore off her bikini top. Her tiny hands tried to hide her penthouse-worthy breasts but failed. He laughed, amused at the fear in the blonde's eyes.

His erection sprung to life, and he forced the girl into position. He placed his cock between her huge breasts and looked at her, expecting her to know what to do next. She gulped, and tears welled up in her eyes as she enclosed his throbbing dick with her huge breasts. After a few minutes, he ordered her to stop. Puzzled, the girl looked up at him.

He smiled when he saw the relief in her eyes. He shook his head, and with hands digging into either side of her waist, he lifted her up and settled her onto his lap, his cock buried deep inside her. He felt her tense around it.

She wriggled, trying to escape, but the movement only heightened his excitement. She managed to squirm her way off him once, but he grabbed her again and roughly put her back in position. The girl stopped wriggling—Baldwin knew she was hoping he'd back off, but he hadn't finished his game, yet. His irritation intensified; he gripped her shoulders as his thrusts gathered momentum and strength. He could feel her insides ripping apart.

"*Non, s'il vous plait, non!*" she shrieked, tears coursing down her reddened cheeks.

"Ah, *oui, chérie. Oui.*"

He stood and moved to the edge of the steamer, the terrified girl wedged in place with his cock still impaled in her. He continued thrusting into her, holding her around her waist to ensure she couldn't escape him. He walked over to the side of the boat and pinned the girl's back to the metal railing to keep her in place.

More tears ran, useless tears that only increased his hatred for her.

Driven, his hands clawed at her throat. Her eyes bulged, and she pleaded in her own language for him to stop. But he ignored her, continued to thrust and choke, his eyes tightly closed in concentration. He choked her and thrust into her, until he climaxed for the second time.

When he opened his eyes, the girl's head had flopped to the side, her tongue lolling out of her mouth. He pulled himself out and casually slung the girl over the side of the boat. Her lifeless body hit the water with a loud splash.

Seconds later, Baldwin was reclining on the steamer, acting as if he didn't have a care in the world. Julio arrived on deck, out of breath, his eyes searching.

"Problem, Julio?"

"Umm, boss… Where's the gi—?"

"Where's the girl? Oh, she fancied a swim." He laughed.

Julio ran to the side of the boat—first the port, then the starboard. His gaze locked on to the naked girl lying face down in the water.

A scream made both men turn. The other girl looked petrified and visibly shaken. Julio moved to comfort her, but Baldwin threw out an arm, blocking his way. "You've had your fun with her, now get rid."

"What?"

"You heard me, unless her fucking screaming has made you deaf. Get fucking rid of her. Now."

Chapter Twenty-Three

Despite Michel telling Lorne and Tony that their moonlight adventure would be discussed over breakfast the next morning, it wasn't mentioned at all. The four sat around the breakfast table, glaring at each other in a stony silence. But then, at nine, true to Michel's word, a car arrived and drove them back to Charles de Gaulle Airport.

Lorne had tried talking to Michel in the reception of the hotel, but it proved to be a waste of time. She had only tried once, as the hatred filling his eyes had pierced her heart and left her wondering how she could have ended up in bed with such a cold, heartless man. She shuddered when she thought that only a few hours before, she had compared him to Jacques, the love of her life. How foolish and misguided could one woman be?

Tony spent the two-and-a-half hour flight back to London lost in his thoughts—which was a relief, for Lorne. It meant she didn't have to worry about empty apologies or banal conversation, and left her free to concentrate on her own confused thoughts.

After finding his car in the vast airport car park, Tony drove Lorne home. Since eating breakfast five hours ago, they'd barely spoken a word to each other.

Finally, as he pulled up outside her house, Lorne had had enough. "I get the impression you blame me for this, Tony."

"For what?"

"Don't give me that crap. You know exactly what I'm talking about."

"As it happens, I'd say it was fifty-fifty."

"How the hell do you work that one out? It was your plan that got us kicked out of France."

"My plan? Oh was that it, now?"

She turned to look at him, her nostrils flaring with rage. "What the fuck is that supposed to mean, *agent boy*?"

His eyes narrowed as she called him that nickname again. "I have no doubt my plan was partially to blame, but if…"

"Oh, don't you dare stop there. Let's have it, smart arse. I've had one of the worst journeys of my life stuck with someone I thought was a friend, who totally ignored me for five hours. Come on. Lay it on the table." She had a feeling what Tony was going to say and prepared herself for the onslaught, her fists clenched till her knuckles turned white.

Tony stared ahead of him, and she followed his gaze to watch a mini trying to reverse into a space twice the size needed for the car and still managing to cock it up. "I said it was fifty-fifty. Yes, I screwed up the plan—well, kind of. I've still got some evidence we can work on, but if you…" He paused, to watch the mini screw up its second attempt to park, and Lorne bashed his thigh with her clenched fist, urging him to continue. "All right; all right. Maybe, if you hadn't slept with the guy, things wouldn't have gotten out of hand."

He had a point, she'd told herself the same thing more than a few hundred times during their journey, but she had no intention of admitting that to him. "That's utter rubbish, and you know it, Tony."

"Is it? If he hadn't gone looking for an encore, he wouldn't have known we were missing, would he?"

"Did he say he'd come to my room last night?"

"No…but—"

"There you have it, Tony. No. For all we know, he might have had the receptionist keeping an eye on us. Here's a novel suggestion for you: He might've even telephoned your room with a query about the case."

"I doubt either one of those scenarios is correct, Lorne."

"Why? Because it's always the women who screw up, isn't it?"

"Bingo, hon. But they don't just screw up; they screw around too—"

Lorne slapped him, hard, across the face. A red mark appeared instantly, and her hand tingled. She couldn't help wondering what was wrong with him, why he felt the need to be judge and jury about the way she led her life.

Or maybe there was another underlying reason behind his vicious, accusing words. Maybe a past girlfriend or his wife had done the dirty on him. If that was the case, maybe he was the type of guy who tarred all women with the same brush.

"I'm sorry, Tony. That was uncalled for," she whispered.

He shrugged and continued to watch the mini try to park for the fourth time. When that didn't work, the driver revved the engine and set off down the road. "Obviously a woman driver," he said, his dry sense of humour trying to break the tension.

"It's bound to be, if my parking is anything to go by." She chuckled.

"I rest my case. I apologise. You had every right to hit me. I allowed my past to cloud my judgement, and that should never have happened."

So she was right: He had struck out at her because of a past experience. Her interest piqued. "Do you want to talk about it?"

He shook his head and patted her leg. "Let me do some digging, and I'll get back to you in a few days."

"Digging into what?"

"Aren't you intrigued to know what those murdered men were doing in France? I'm not satisfied with what Amore dug up, so I'm off to HQ to do some digging of my own."

"But he didn't dig *anything* up on those guys."

"Precisely. That seems odd to me. I'll get back to you later, okay?" He stepped out of the car to retrieve her overnight bag from the boot. She joined him, apologised again for hitting him, took her bag, then turned and walked up the path to her home.

The air in the car had been frosty, but it was nothing compared to how cold the house felt when she stepped through the front door. Lorne walked through to the kitchen and turned up the heat. Then she boiled the kettle and poured herself a mug of coffee.

Feeling warmer, she went back to the lounge to ring her father. "Hi, Dad. It's me."

"Lorne, how are you, sweetheart? More to the point, where are you?"

It was a relief to hear how happy he seemed to hear her voice. In the background, she heard Henry whimpering. "I'm fine, and I'm home. Is that my boy, I hear?"

"That's the pest, yes. And you, my girl, sound tired. Have you just got back?"

"Yep, I thought I'd ring you first. All right if I pick 'pest' up in the morning, Dad?" Lorne was desperate to see her dog, and Tony would take at least a few days to get back with her.

He let out an exaggerated sigh. She chortled.

"I suppose so. What time?"

"I'll be there nice and early, so don't bother taking him out first thing. See you about nine."

"That's half the morning gone by then, girl. Old Henry has been waking me up at seven, expecting his daily walk. You have a lie-in, love. I'll take him tomorrow; it'll be a farewell gift from me. Come round about twelve, and we'll go and have a nice pub lunch at the Harvester down the road, my treat."

"Thanks, Dad. You're a real gem. See you tomorrow. Give Henry a cuddle and kiss from me."

"I'll do no such thing. If I've told you once, I've told you a dozen times: It ain't right to kiss a dog, not when they lick their own... Well, you know what I mean."

She laughed. "Till tomorrow, Dad." A quick sip of coffee gave her enough courage to tackle the next person or persons on her 'to ring' list.

"Hello... Who's speaking? And what do you want?"

Lorne rolled her eyes when she heard the voice of her forthright fourteen-year-old daughter. "Well, at least you had the courtesy to say 'hello' before you started your interrogation."

"Mum... Where are you? Can I come and stay? Did you bring me a gift?"

"It's good to hear your voice too, sweetheart. I'm back home. Sorry—I didn't have time to pick up a gift—and sorry again—no, you can't come and stay. It's a school night, and your father and I agreed that you could only visit at the weekend."

Lorne expected the teenager to groan and throw a tantrum, but she didn't. Maybe the doctor was doing a better job than anyone gave her credit for. "Worth a try, huh, Mum? You know what they say, 'God loves a trier.' Can I see you at the weekend then, Mum... Please?"

"I don't see why not, hon. Is your father there?"

Instead of handing the phone over to her father, Charlie prattled on for several minutes about the latest celebrity gossip she'd read in her girly magazine, before moving on to what had happened in the soaps that week. Lorne found it impossible to get a word in edgeways. Finally, an out-of-breath Charlie passed the phone to her father.

When she heard Tom's voice, Lorne's stomach tangled in knots, and she didn't have a clue why. Any love she'd had for him had long since disappeared. Maybe she was still feeling tense after the argument with Tony.

"Lorne?"

"Hi, Tom. How's things?"

"Like you care. What do you want, Lorne? I'm busy."

Same old Tom: snappy, impatient, and to the point. "I'm sorry for interrupting you. Is it all right if Charlie stays the weekend?"

"Oh, you mean like last weekend? Oh no, that's right—you cancelled at the last minute."

She closed her eyes, placed her hand over the mouthpiece, and expelled a long sigh. *Here we go again. Christ, if ever there was a doubt why I divorced you, you've just put paid to that, mate.* "Circumstances out of my control, Tom. I had to deal with something that simply couldn't wait."

"Such as?"

"Sorry, Tom. That's personal, and as we're no longer married—"

"Not that you ever told me what you were up to when we were married. That *frog* comes to mind."

Jesus, not that old chestnut. She bit her tongue and refused to be goaded. "A simple yes or no will suffice, Tom."

"Yes."

The phone went dead. She went into the kitchen to make an omelette and found herself shaking her head in frustration all through the preparation, cooking, and consumption of it. *Men. Why the hell do I bother with them!*

Chapter Twenty-Four

The following morning at eleven thirty, Lorne arrived at her father's house. Hoping no one would notice her, she hurried down the side alley to peer over the fence. She had a feeling if she turned up early she would find her father playing with 'the pest'.

Jackpot! Bursting through the gate, she shouted, "Hah! Caught you!"

Sam Collins collapsed into a nearby deckchair. His hand flew up to his chest, and he gasped for breath. "Jeez, Lorne... You nearly gave me a heart attack... Why didn't you come in the front way?"

"Oh, Dad, are you all right? I thought I'd catch you two out." Henry recovered from the fright more quickly than her father did and bounded towards her, almost knocking her to the ground in the process. "Hello, munchkin. Did you miss your mummy?"

The dog answered by running in the opposite direction, only to return a few moments later with the soggy bone-shaped toy that had driven her father round the twist the last few days. Henry dropped the toy at her feet and barked expectantly.

"Cut it out. What have I told you about not barking, pest?" Sam chastised the dog, by the laughter Lorne saw in his eyes, he didn't mean his harsh words.

"He loves his mum—don't you, bud?"

"Come on. Enough of this. I need a drink. Let's go to the pub before it gets too busy. You can stay here, mutt." He added, as Henry trotted after them.

When they walked into the pub, Lorne was delighted to see her sister Jade sitting at a table, holding her baby son. After hugging and kissing each other, Lorne took little Gino from Jade, while their father went to the bar to buy the drinks. "How's the little guy doing?" Lorne asked as she kissed and nuzzled the baby's neck, loving the comforting smell she found.

"He's getting there. The hospital is pleased with his progress. They're monitoring his heart. Sometimes he gets out of breath easy, but they say that's normal."

"You look shattered, sweetie."

Jade shrugged. Her brown shoulder-length hair had a kink in it, so it had been left to dry naturally that morning. Lorne also noted that her sister was wearing barely any makeup—which was almost unheard of and it did little to disguise the dark circles under Jade's eyes. "The joys of motherhood, eh?"

"Are you sure that's all it is, Jade?" Lorne looked deep in her sister's eyes and saw a spark lying within. "Come on. What's up?"

"Christ, once a cop always a cop, hey, sis? There are two things, actually. One is..." Jade looked over at the bar, making sure their father was still busy. "I'm pregnant. You're the first to know, and I'd like to keep it that way for the time being. Luigi and I aren't sure if we're going to keep the baby. You know, after what we've been through with little Gino, we're wondering if it would be fair to put another child through all that. The doctors say it's too early to tell if the baby has the same heart defect."

Bouncing Gino on her knee, Lorne stretched a hand across the table to cover her sister's. "How awful. I mean, of course, I'm pleased for you, but what a dilemma for you both. All I can say is, take your time and don't make any rash decisions you might regret later. Any choice you make, you know you'll have my full backing, hon."

"Thanks, Lorne, and... The second thing is, Judith rang me a few days ago."

Lorne's attention turned to Gino again, and she bounced him harder on her knee, while she struggled to search for an answer to the question she knew her sister was going to ask next.

"Lorne? What's going on? You *never* lie. Come on. Tell me where you've been and why you involved Judith—her name, at least—knowing that she rings me regularly?"

It was Lorne's turn to cast her eyes over at the bar to see how far her father had progressed in the queue. She could've kicked herself for using their friend Judith as an excuse. In her haste, she had forgotten how close Jade and Judith were, especially since they'd both had babies within a few weeks of each other. Now, she had a dilemma of her own to solve. Did she confide in Jade about where she had disappeared to, knowing the amount of stress her sister was already under, or did she tell another lie and risk being caught out again by her astute sister?

"I don't want to worry you, hon. You've got enough on your plate at the moment."

Jade took the baby from Lorne and settled him into the high chair next to her. "Lorne, when Mum died, we made a promise that we'd never keep secrets from each other. I've just lived up to my side of the bargain by telling you about the baby, now spill."

Lorne's gaze dropped to the table. She picked up the salt and pepper pots in front of her and started twirling them on the table. "He's back," she whispered.

"Sorry?"

Lorne looked her sister in the eye. In a much louder voice, she said, "He's back, Jade." She watched Jade's expression change, ranging from puzzlement to comprehension in quick succession.

"Who's back?" her father asked, setting the three glasses down on the table.

Shit, shit, shit! Damn my big mouth!

Lorne's silence, coupled with his experience as a former Chief Inspector in the Met, meant it didn't take her father long to work out whom she was talking about. He sat down heavily in the seat opposite her, the colour draining from his face. "You're kidding. Where? When? More to the point, why?"

Lorne recounted the drama she and Tony had been through the past few days—or, at least ninety percent of it.

"So you never went to Judith's, then."

"No, Dad. Please forgive me for lying, Tony turned up and—"

Her father banged his fist on the table. "Tony had no right to involve you in this, Lorne. You're out of the game, now."

"I know, Dad, but he remembered what I said to him last year when we got Charlie back—you know, about me wanting revenge. Well, he kind of took me at my word."

"So what happens now?"

"I don't know. The last I heard, Tony was going to go digging for dirt. It depends what he digs up, I suppose."

Sam reached a bony hand across the table and gripped hers. "Please, Lorne, promise me… Promise me you won't get involved."

Lorne's gaze rose to her father's. He looked tired and old, and she regretted how much pain her following words would cause him, but the regret didn't stop her from shaking her head and saying. "I can't do that, Dad."

Chapter Twenty-Five

Lunch turned out to be one of the quietest Lorne had ever spent with Jade and her father At times, she thought each of them had became lost in their own deep scary thoughts, reliving the horrors of the previous year. They parted soon after eating their meal, which was a rarity.

On the way home, Lorne stopped off at the park to give Henry an extra run, to make up for deserting him the way she had. The detour also gave her some much-needed time to clear her head.

She watched the eight-year-old dog run around with the boundless energy of a two-year-old person, but she didn't succeed in clearing the turmoil going on in her mind.

Lorne arrived home and spent the next four hours cleaning the house from top to bottom, which she only tended to do when her mind wouldn't shut down, so she knew then that she was in big trouble. After a quick sandwich, she settled down to an evening in front of the telly, making sure she avoided the soaps, aware that Charlie would fill her in on those at the weekend during her visit.

At around nine, her mind was churning so much that she decided to get her thoughts down on paper.

1. The Unicorn/Baldwin—why has he resurfaced in France?

2. Why is he out in the open and not living under an assumed name? He knows there is an active arrest warrant awaiting him, albeit in England.

3. Why were the murdered Finance Ministers in Normandy?

4. Why had they held a meeting with Baldwin?

5. Why Normandy? Why not the South of France?

6. Why did I sleep with Michel?

7. Is there more to Michel than meets the eye? Did he really grow up around Normandy?

8. Why? Why? Why? Did I tell Jade about Baldwin, only for Dad to overhear?

9. And why the heck am I making notes about a case I don't want to get involved in?

Deep in thought, she almost hit the ceiling when the phone rang. "Hello?" She ruffled the top of Henry's head as she answered.

"Ah, Lorne. You've arrived back home safe and well, I see." A haunting laugh travelled down the line.

Lorne closed her eyes and broke out in a cold sweat, but she forced herself to remain calm and in control. It had been a whole year since she'd last heard the goading voice. She placed a hand over the mouthpiece and blew out a breath, then responded nonchalantly, "Baldwin, what do you want?"

"You disappoint me, Insp… Oops, can't call you that anymore, can I? You disappoint me, *Lorne*."

She shuddered as her name was drawn out by his poisonous tongue. "In what way?"

"You and your agent boyfriend gave up so easily, not what I expected at all. Especially after the way you threatened me—well, some might call it a threat. I, on the other hand, would say it was more like an anguished cry of revenge by a *very* desperate woman."

"For a start, Tony is *not* my boyfriend, and I assure you: I will carry out my threat, one day. After all, I've allocated a special place on my desk for your gonads. I'm in need of a new paperweight." She amazed herself by pushing away the fear and replacing it with the feistiness she'd always shown the criminal.

His laughter filled her ear. "I see your fighting spirit is still intact despite the losses you've incurred, dear lady."

Don't give in to him, Lorne. Stay strong and calm. "That's one thing you haven't been able to take from me, Baldwin, and I doubt you ever will."

"Hmm… That sounds like a challenge to me."

She heard him smack his lips and shuddered again. She was used to him playing mind games with her, but she didn't feel nervous, because she knew he was in France. *Or is he?* Did he follow her back to England? No, she doubted that, doubted he had the balls to enter the country, knowing that he would be arrested if he came anywhere near the UK.

"Like I said: What do you want, Baldwin?"

"I see your patience hasn't improved any since your retirement. This time, nothing, except to give you one final warning, Lorne: *Back off.* And get your agent boyfriend to back off, too. Otherwise…"

All Lorne heard next was the dial tone.

As her anger deepened, she threw the phone across the room, just managing to miss the TV in the corner. Thinking the phone was one of his toys, Henry trotted over to it, picked it up in his mouth, and returned to her, placing it gently in her lap.

Despite feeling like shit, she smiled down at him. "Where would I be without my faithful companion to brighten my day?"

Picking up her pen, she added a few more questions to the list:

10. Why does Baldwin still want to make my life hell?

11. What is it going to take to get rid of the bastard once and for all?

Chapter Twenty-Six

Lorne woke at eight on Friday morning, feeling perkier than she'd felt in a year. Did Baldwin's phone call have something to do with that? Or had her trip to France, especially the trip to the cemetery, forced her to push on with her life and to put the past behind her?

After walking Henry, she popped down to Waitrose; her kitchen cupboards were bare, and she needed to stock up on food for the weekend. Charlie was a typical teenager, a regular human dustbin. From the minute Charlie stepped foot in Lorne's house on a Friday evening, the fridge contents were under attack. God knew where the girl put it–there wasn't an ounce of excess weight on her bones.

As Lorne finished adding a layer of grated cheese to the cottage pie she'd rustled up for dinner, the phone rang. She hesitated before answering it, not recognising the number on the display. She took a deep breath. "Hello?"

"I need you to pack a bag."

"Tony?"

"Unless you have a secret lover—correction, *another* secret lover—you're not telling me about, who else would be ringing you up to tell you to pack a bag?"

"Full of wise-arse statements aren't you, agent boy?"

"And you're intent on making me your enemy, Lorne, if you keep calling me that."

She smiled and imagined him pulling all sorts of faces at his end. "Anyway, hon, that's a negative."

"What's a negative?"

"Me packing a bag. I have Charlie coming for the weekend, and after letting her down last week, I can't—no, I *won't*—do it again."

"You're kidding, right? Winding me up?"

"Nope."

Lorne heard him blow out a frustrated sigh and waited for the backlash. "Hey, Lorne, the kid will understand. You can make it up to her in the future. You have a lifetime to make it up to her."

"You know what, Tony? I can tell you haven't got any kids. My life wouldn't be worth living if I let her down two weeks in a row.

And furthermore, I'm in a lifetime of debt to the girl already after what Baldwin did to her."

"Point taken with regard to last year, but—"

"No 'but's, Tony. Not this time."

"Guess you're not interested in what I found out, then?"

"I didn't say that. Oh, and just to let you know, Baldwin knows we're on his tail."

"How the heck do you know that? Oh, wait a minute. Been talking to *froggie,* have we?"

Lorne held the portable phone between her head and shoulder as she sliced up the tomatoes to go on top of the dinner she'd slaved over for the past hour and a half. Tutting loudly, she said, "You're such an arsehole at times. No, it wasn't Michel who told me. I actually heard it from the horse's mouth."

Silence answered her.

"Tony?"

"Did I hear you right? Baldwin's made contact with you?"

"Yes and yes. He told me it was my final warning, and that you and I should back off."

"Don't you see, Lorne? You'll have to come with me now."

She placed the casserole dish in the oven and headed to the lounge. "How do you work that one out? And the answer is still no, by the way."

"He's obviously worried. Otherwise, why would he contact you after all this time?"

"I don't know, and I don't care. Not before the weekend, anyway. End of. Now, tell me what you managed to find out?"

"No way, José. You either come with me, or I withhold the details. The choice is yours."

"Tell you what, Tony: Go play your futile games with someone who cares." She pressed the *End Call* button on the phone. *Bullying jerk. Who the hell does he think he is?*

Before she had the chance to pick up her magazine, the phone rang again. Seeing that it was the same number, she waited. Finally, after twenty rings, she answered it but didn't speak.

"You care, Lorne. I know you do. I'm sorry for not thinking about Charlie, but I have information, good information, and if we don't get back to France immediately, I can't see another opportunity arising for us to nab the bastard."

"Clarify?"

"When we're in France."

"So it's something big, then?"

"It's big, all right. Far bigger than any of the stunts he's pulled off in the past."

Jesus, he sure knew how to gain her attention. Could she go back to France so soon? Could she let Charlie down again? As she mulled over the questions, the little voice in her head replayed Baldwin's goading voice—not only the conversation she'd had with him the night before, but the night he'd pulled the trigger on Jacques, too. Goading, taunting, warning her to back off and not to interfere.

Then she found herself thinking, *You've never listened to Baldwin before, so why should you listen to him now?*

She let out a long resigned breath. "When do we leave?"

"I've booked us on the nine-fifteen leaving Heathrow. Make sure you pack only the essentials."

"How many days?"

"Hmmm… I'd say at least a week."

"A week! Tony, I have a dog to think about. I can't keep farming him out."

"Not my problem, Lorne. I'll pick you up at seven on the dot."

That gave her five hours to drop Henry off at her father's again, pack a bag, and call Charlie to apologise—again. Lorne worked her way backwards through the list. Charlie was still at school, and Tom had been called out on a breakdown at work. So, she chose the coward's way out and left a message—a very apologetic message—on their answer-phone.

She ran upstairs, emptied out the overnight bag she hadn't even unpacked from their last trip, and stuffed it with T-shirts, skinny jeans, a few jumpers and underwear. Then she ran into the bathroom and gathered up her toiletries, adding them to the bag.

A few minutes later, she was in the car, en route to her father's house with Henry in the back, his head hung low. *Jesus, 'Psychic dog' strikes again. He knows exactly where he's going and what's happening.* "I promise I'll make it up to you, boy."

"Lorne?" Her father looked puzzled when the pair appeared in the rear garden of his semi-detached house.

"Hi, Dad… Umm, I need to ask a big favour."

Sam Collins shook his head. "Not if you're going back to France, I'm not."

"Dad, please. I need to do this."

Her father tore off his gardening gloves, threw them on the bed of geraniums he'd been weeding, and stomped in the house. Lorne knew she had a battle on her hands and needed to think fast on her feet. Time was running out.

Following her father into the house, she found him sitting at the kitchen table with his head in his hands. Her heart sank. She went over to him and wrapped an arm around his shoulders. "Dad, please."

"Lorne, let it go. I know you've been in limbo since...*it* happened, but it's time to move on to pastures new, love. Forget about the Unicorn and start living your life again."

"Dad, I understand what you're saying, and I know I've been a cow recently—but surely, even you can understand that I need to find closure." He looked up at her, tears welling and threatening to fall. She squeezed his shoulder tightly and continued, "You know I have to do this, Dad, don't you?"

He nodded, and a tear slipped onto his wrinkled cheek. "If I was in your shoes, I'd want the same. I wouldn't give up either, but what kind of father would I be if I didn't try to dissuade you? Let the authorities sort it out, girl."

"I'll let you into a secret, Dad: I woke up this morning feeling like I could take on the world. That's the first time in over a year I've felt like that. I feel invigorated, as if my life suddenly has a purpose. If I promise to be careful and to ring you every day at a certain time, would that help?"

He studied her carefully. "Your eyes do appear to have some life in them at last, but what happens if he finally kills you? How do you think that will make me feel, knowing that I gave you my blessing to go back there?"

"He won't get me, Dad. I'll get *him*. Tony is an experienced agent. He won't let anything happen to me."

"So this will be a covert operation, I take it?"

"Yes, Dad."

Her father shook his head, and with his elbows on the table, leaned his forehead on the heels of his hands. "Good God, that's even worse, Lorne. No one will know where you are, if you get into any danger over there," he mumbled.

"Wrong, Dad. You'll know every step we make."

As her words sunk in, he sat upright, his spine straightening as he pulled his shoulders back. He glanced down at Henry, who was quietly sitting with his head on the old man's lap. He patted the dog's head. "Guess we're stuck with each other, pal."

Lorne flung her arms around her father's neck and kissed his face half a dozen times. "Oh, Dad, you're an angel."

"Not yet, I'm not. Go on. Off with you. The boy will be all right with me. When's your flight. I take it you are flying out?"

"Tony's picking me up at seven." She checked her watch and gulped. *Half an hour!*

"Jeez, Lorne, you better go. Take care, girl. Ring me at nine on the dot every night. If I don't hear from you, I'll call the authorities—if I can make myself understood, that is."

"I will, Dad. Nine o'clock on the dot—and thanks. You two take good care of each other. I'll be back soon, if not sooner." Lorne stepped out the front door and shouted over her shoulder, "Love you."

Chapter Twenty-Seven

Tony picked her up at seven. "Well?" she asked, before she'd even closed the car door.

"Can I at least put the car into gear before you start interrogating me?"

She blew out the breath she'd been holding in. She waited another five minutes before she tried again. "C'mon, Tony. you can be so frustrating at times."

"And you, dear lady, can be so impatient at times. It's all in my bag. Difficult to show you when I'm driving."

"There's no need to show me, just bloody tell me!' She looked at him through narrowed eyes and thought he looked kind of shifty. He was avoiding eye contact and only focusing on the road ahead of him, which led her to think maybe he had tricked her into going back to France with him. *No, he wouldn't be as underhanded as that, would he?*

Silence.

Her suspicions grew. "Tony?"

He sighed heavily and winced. "You really shouldn't have retired, Lorne."

"You utter bastard. You've tricked me. Just who the hell do you think you are? I don't know who's worse, you or Baldwin."

"Hey, now. That's a bit over the top. Yes, I may have *misled* you slightly, but you'll thank me in the end, of that I'm certain."

Her hands clenched and unclenched in her lap. "So you found out nothing, I take it?"

"Ah, now that's where you'd be wrong. MI6 have been working around the clock since the two bodies were found. They're just putting together the final pieces of the puzzle, and they should be completed in the next day or so. So, I thought it would make sense for us to be in France ready and waiting, for when the go-ahead comes through."

She had to agree his logic did sound feasible, but it still didn't stop her objections to being lied to. Sadness filled her as she said quietly, "I hope you're satisficd, Agent Warner, because I think your lies may have cost me my relationship with my daughter."

He didn't reply, but she did hear him gulp, and the rest of the journey remained silent.

In the departure lounge, Tony broke the chill between them first, asking Lorne if she'd like a drink. Her refusal came out sharper than intended, and he left her to sulk while he browsed the shops surrounding the seating area.

When they boarded the plane, Tony handed her a peace offering: a lollipop with a sad clown's face etched on it.

She laughed and punched his upper arm, hard. "Idiot! Where are we going to stay when we get there?"

"I've arranged to pick up a hire car. We'll drive to Caen and find a small hotel or guest house when we arrive."

"Wouldn't it be better to stay in Paris tonight and drive to Caen tomorrow in the daylight?" Her watch read eleven thirty. They were due to land at midnight. "If I remember, it's a two-and-a-half hour trip to Caen. That means it'll be almost three before we get there."

"You see, Sherlock? I knew there was a reason I wanted you to accompany me on this trip."

His sarcasm earned him another thump in the arm. "You men. Just have problems working out the finer details. You know, the practical issues: where to stay, what to eat, what to pack, how to be *honest*."

"Ouch, okay, you've made your point. Women are truly indispensable." He laughed, and for the first time Lorne noticed how the scar on his face appeared less prominent when he smiled and how white his teeth were when they weren't covered by his thin lips.

They managed to locate a cheap hotel close to the airport and booked a double room with twin beds due to Tony's budget restraints. Lorne—and evidently Tony, as well—lacked the time or the energy to feel any discomfort at sharing, and they each collapsed into a bed soon after their arrival.

The alarm went off at six the next morning, and after grabbing a quick coffee and croissant, they set off for Normandy.

Lorne asked, "Are we going to book into a hotel first?"

"No. I thought we'd take a trip out to Baldwin's chateau."

She turned her head sharply. "You mean we're going out there in the daylight. Why? What do you hope to achieve?"

"You never let up with the damn questions, do you? Obviously, we're not going to drive up to the chateau, like our *froggie* colleagues. We'll need to be more discreet than that. I want to see what kind of mischief these guys get up to during the day. I'd like to find out why he has an army of men surrounding him. He's never had that many around him before, has he?"

She shrugged and shook her head. "I seem to remember that on his last job, he had about four guys in tow, and that was considered a big job. Was it four or three? He shot one, and two ended up in prison, but I think there was another guy, too. I'm not sure, though."

"That's my point. We regarded the job a year ago as large, so if he's employing twenty men now, this must be a *huge* job. I just wish our guys would pull their fingers out and find out something concrete."

"You never did say about the file you copied at the chateau, if it came up trumps."

"It was as I suspected: a list of art that has been stolen over the last year, and it tallies up with Interpol's database."

"So, if we told the *capitaine* about the list, he could challenge Baldwin about it, couldn't he?"

Tony blew out a breath. "I doubt it. I know you don't want to hear this, Lorne, but I genuinely believe he's involved with Baldwin. Everything points to that, even the way we approached the chateau by posse, only to find Baldwin off the premises. Jesus, Baldwin hasn't even been pulled in for questioning. There's just no urgency where the *capitaine*'s concerned, which leads me to believe he's dragging his feet. Why would he do that, if he wasn't going to gain from it?"

Lorne had trouble holding back the feeling of shame eating at her. She had found it so easy opening up to the *capitaine* that evening in her room, and now she couldn't help thinking that he'd tricked her. Had he used his French charm to find out what she knew about Baldwin?

She'd felt an affinity with Michel because of who he had been: one of Jacque's best friends. Maybe that had been a ruse, too. She wondered if Tony might be right, but a small part of her clung to hope: *He might be wrong, too.*

"Lorne?"

"Hmm… Sorry. I was miles away. You know that the jury is still out for me on that one, Tony. And no, before you say it, it's not because I slept with the guy."

"I wasn't about to say anything of the sort. He caught you at a low ebb, and you needed to reach out to someone. I can understand that."

"Why, thank you Mr. Psychoanalyst, for being so understanding. I guess we'll have to agree to differ on that one for the time being until we stumble across evidence to the contrary."

"Fair enough." He added cheekily, "I'll bet you a hundred notes, though."

"In case you hadn't noticed, Tony, I'm one of the unemployed—and no, I don't draw benefits. I still have a little put by from the sale of the house, but I need that money to finish off my garden. Then I'll make finding a job my number one priority."

"I've told you before: Join MI5—or better still, come and join me at MI6. At least you'll see the world."

"Yeah, and even less of my family. We'll see. I might even carry on property developing. I'm good at it, if that doesn't sound too boastful."

"By what I saw of your new house, you could be right, but then there's the downturn in the housing market to consider, plus the dire straits of the economy. I can't see the banks rushing to lend people money at the moment. Just be careful."

"We'll talk more when this is over. We're coming up to the turnoff now. I'm going to drive past, see where the neighbour's property starts, and go through that way." He glanced down at her trainers. "Glad to see you're wearing suitable footwear."

The adjoining property turned out to be a farm. He drove the car down a muddy dirt track. Using the trees as cover, they made their way over the fields to the chateau.

Lorne pulled on Tony's arm as he went to step into an open field. "Hold on a minute. How do you know this isn't Baldwin's land?"

They crouched down and surveyed the open bronze-coloured field ahead of them. "You're right, but look." He pointed out the large bales of straw stacked at one end of the field. "You can smell it's recently been cut."

"Meaning?"

"You really have been out of the game too long. Meaning that the field must belong to the farmer, because if Baldwin owned it, he wouldn't want anyone snooping around."

They ran across the next field, towards the outline of the chateau beyond, stopping at a hedgerow where they assessed their route again. The field was lush and green and full of cows munching on the foot-high grass.

After going over a further two fields, they found themselves about a hundred feet or so behind the chateau. Tony looked through his binoculars and searched the area in every direction.

"What do you see?" Lorne asked impatiently.

He didn't respond for several minutes. "I can just make out the tail end of a lorry. The sides are up. I need to move further that way to get a better view."

They stooped and ran along the boundary to get to a better position. Once they stopped, Tony locked the binoculars onto the vehicle again. "Jesus…"

"What?" Lorne took the binoculars when Tony offered them. "Oh my God! There must be dozens of pictures in there."

Tony snatched back the binoculars and continued to scan the immediate area around the lorry. "I count maybe fifteen men, all built like the Incredible Hulk."

"Are they loading or unloading the vehicle?"

"It's hard to tell at the moment. Looks like they're having a break. Wait a minute—Baldwin has just come out of the chateau. He's ranting about something; the men are returning to work. They're unloading *and* loading."

"Then we call the police, Tony. Let them deal with it."

"And tell them what, Lorne? For all we know, this could be a legitimate delivery."

She thumped herself in the thigh. "But we know what the likelihood of that is, don't we?"

"Come on. Think about it. What would you do if you received a call from some foreigners telling you that a delivery was being made?"

"Okay, point taken. Sorry I spoke. What are we going to do, then?"

"We sit, wait, and observe—till nightfall, if we have to."

Chapter Twenty-Eight

Not long after receiving a rocket up their arses, his men seemed to move up a gear; within a few hours, they'd loaded the lorry and were heading towards the motorway.

Tony and Lorne booked into a charming little chambre d'hôte around six PM still buzzing from what they'd witnessed.

Lorne pulled the zipper on her overnight bag, ready to unpack her clothes, but Tony stopped her. "I wouldn't do that, if I were you. We'll probably need to leave at the drop of a hat."

"So I have to live out of a suitcase—or canvas bag, I should say? Yeah, that's okay, mate. That'll do wonders for my image, walking around in creased clothes." She stomped into the bathroom with her toiletry bag tucked under her arm before he had the chance to retaliate.

Lorne spent the next half hour soaking in a hot bubble bath, her eyes closed. She ran the soap slowly up her legs, along her arms, over her neck. Then she imagined her hands were the *capitaine*'s, and she moved down to caress her breasts and nipples. A smile tugged at her lips and her heart rate accelerated when her hands slipped into the water and soaped between her legs, fingers searching, almost bringing her to the verge of—

Her eyes flew open. *Damn it! What's wrong with you, woman? That night with him was a mistake, a bloody mistake!*

Lorne dressed and returned back to the bedroom to find Tony sitting at the small dressing table against the far wall, talking to someone on his mobile. She watched as he nodded, expression concerned. He made eye contact with her, smiled briefly, and then continued making notes on the pad in front of him.

Lorne sat on the end of her bed and dried her hair with the towel while she waited for him to finish his call. She noticed a big spider spinning a web in the corner of the room and shuddered. She hated spiders more than she hated Manchester United.

Tony hardly spoke to the person who was calling him, but Lorne did manage to pick out the words *art, finance, gold, accounts,* and *Monaco.*

Finally, he hung up and sat down on the bed opposite her. He still held the pad in his hands, and he rested his elbows on his knees. "Hmm… Interesting."

"Jesus, here we go again. Anytime you feel like sharing the information with me, Tony, don't hold back."

"Ever tried meditation?"

"What?"

"Apparently it calms a person down and…" He stopped pushing at her scowl. "Okay, here's what the guys have found out. First up, the two men murdered were the Russian and the Chinese Finance Ministers. If my memory serves me right, I think the frog *capitaine* already told us that much. However, he neglected to tell us that the day they flew into France, they were joined by several other Finance Ministers, from every country."

Her mouth dropped open. "Every country?"

"Let's just say every country of note. Why do you think *froggie* kept that from us?"

"Maybe he wasn't aware of it."

"Hmm… I doubt that. He's playing a very dangerous game. I'm surprised the other officers haven't sussed him out by now."

"Like I said, the jury is still out as far as I'm concerned. What else?"

Tony shook his head, then continued, "I was right about the file we found at the chateau. The list matched up to Interpol's stolen art list. I guess we saw the evidence with our own eyes this morning. Talking of this morning, have you got anything to put on those scratches?" He nodded towards the bramble marks on her arms.

"Forgot to pack my first-aid kit. It doesn't matter. I'm sure I'll live. Go on."

Tony sought out his flight bag and returned with a tube of antiseptic, which he handed to her along with a cotton wool pad. Lorne accepted them, surprised that he'd brought first aid.

He shrugged. "Tools of the trade. Anyway, what we need to find out is: Where is the art going? Is Baldwin storing it at the chateau? Is he selling it? From what we saw today, it's obviously a big operation. I just can't believe that so far he's been allowed to get away with it. Surely the locals and Interpol must realise what the guy's up to."

Lorne knew the agent had a valid point. She questioned the *capitaine*'s innocence as she dabbed her forearm with the cream

Tony had given her, wincing a few times when it stung, seeping into the wound. "The more evidence you gather, the likelier it seems that *someone* knows what's going on at that chateau. Whether that someone is Michel remains to be seen. Have your guys come up with anything else? I heard you mention something about gold?"

"Yeah, listen to this: We both know what state the world's economy is in right now, don't we?"

She nodded.

He continued, "Well, it looks like Baldwin is dipping into the world's gold reserves."

"What? How?"

"HQ reckons that's what the meeting was about, the reason behind all the Finance Ministers coming to France. He wants to get his mucky paws on their gold. When HQ started digging and asking questions of those who were present that evening, most of them refused to comment as if they were too scared to. But then they hit the jackpot with the bloke from the Philippines. He said that the evening had started off well—good food, entertainment, and plenty of pretty girls—then things turned sour very quickly."

Lorne raised an eyebrow.

"The murdered men spoke out against Baldwin, refusing to bow to his threats. Before anyone could blink, they were shot in cold blood. We both know how Baldwin's mind works. Looks like his bullying tactics came up trumps this time, too."

"It doesn't make sense. Why would he go after the gold? Where the fuck is he going to put it? And why the hell did he gather the Finance Ministers together in France? And a third question: What the bloody hell does he have over these guys? I take it this involves some kind of blackmail?"

"So the guy from the Philippines says, yeah. Apparently Baldwin's got a dossier on every country's head of state and is threatening to expose them if his demands aren't met. It must've taken him years to think up this scam. The reason this meeting took place in France was because Baldwin wanted to show off his new pad. All these men were personal friends of his."

"He's a cunning little shit. Over the years, he's built up relationships with the men, knowing exactly what roles they played in their respective governments. As far as they were concerned, he sold himself as an influential businessman. Remember, it was only last year that we learned his true identity."

"Jesus, you're right. But what about the gold?"

Tony propped the pillows up against the headboard, removed his shoes, and swung his legs up on the bed. "That's the part HQ is having trouble figuring out. Like you say, where the hell would he store it? It's a complex plan that appears to be working, though."

Lorne settled herself on the other bed, copying Tony's position. "How do you mean?"

"HQ are keeping an eye on these countries accounts, specifically looking for any large transfers heading for the Cayman Islands. So far, £500 million has been transferred."

Lorne swung her legs off the bed and sat on the edge of it. "What? Can't they do anything to stop him? You said pounds, not gold?"

"Yeah, maybe the gold part was a ploy. It appears to be working, anyway. There's no telling how much this guy will swindle out of these countries if we don't stop him.

"Oh, yeah, I forgot one minor detail. He's doing this to fulfil his ambition."

"And that is?"

"To be the world's richest man."

Chapter Twenty-Nine

The following morning, Lorne had Tony's scribbled notes in her hand. The list of questions she'd made back in England lay on the bed beside her.

Tony came out of the bathroom, drying his hair with a towel. He had another towel wrapped around his waist that stopped just short of his toned muscles.

 Lorne cleared her throat and cursed under her breath when her cheeks heated up. "Umm... Here's the list I was telling you about last night." She handed him the sheet of paper when he sat down next to her.

The smell of his aftershave filled her nostrils and set her heart thumping. His body, still damp from his shower, glistened in the sunlight streaming in from the window. *Lorne, he's a colleague—of sorts. Remember, you don't mix business with pleasure!*

Seconds later, her mind fired back, *So what was Michel, then?*

"You have some valid questions here, Lorne. But I'm intrigued to know why you have crossed out number six?"

1. *The Unicorn/Baldwin—why has he resurfaced in France?*
2. *Why is he out in the open and not living under an assumed name? He knows there is an arrest warrant awaiting him, albeit in England.*
3. *Why were the murdered Finance Ministers in Normandy?*
4. *Why had they held a meeting with Baldwin?*
5. *Why Normandy? Why not the South of France?*
6. ~~*Why did I sleep with Michel?*~~
7. *Is there more to Michel than meets the eye? Did he really grow up around Normandy.*
8. *Why? Why? Why? Did I tell Jade about Baldwin only for Dad to overhear.*
9. *And why the heck am I making notes about a case I don't want to get involved in?*

10. Why did Baldwin still want to make my life hell?

11. What is it going to take to get rid of the bastard once and for all?

Her cheeks got hotter, and she snatched the list from his grasp. With her pen, she scribbled through number six until it was totally obliterated, then handed the list back to him.

"Guess that answers my question." He chuckled.

His quip sent her scurrying into the bathroom, where she studied her reflection in the mirror above the sink. She scowled at herself and whispered, "Get a grip, Lorne. You *will* keep control of your emotions. One foolish assignation in France is enough. Put those defences back up and be professional."

After a quick shower, she stepped back into the bedroom wearing only a towel. Relief flooded her when she found Tony fully dressed. Neither of them said a word as she rummaged through her bag, picking out the clothes she intended to wear, and went back in the bathroom.

She re-entered the bedroom ten minutes later, dressed and with her equilibrium fully restored. "What are we going to do about breakfast? I'm starving."

Tony's gaze glinted with understanding. He picked up both documents from the bed and stuffed them in a file folder. He put the file in his bag and propped it up against the wall before heading towards the door. "You dry your hair. I'll have a quick recce; be back in five."

Fifteen minutes later, they sat in a small café, eating freshly baked *pain au chocolat* and croissants. Lorne had dipped into Tony's bag to retrieve the file and brought it with her. She had it open, studying his notes.

Gold reserves held by each country.
China $1,534,000,000,000
Japan $ 954,100,000,000
Russia $476,400,000,000
India $275,000,000,000
Taiwan $274,000,000,000
South Korea $262,200,000,000
Brazil $180,300,000,000

Germany $136,200,000,000
France $98,240,000,000
Italy $94,330,000,000
UK $57,300,000,000

"How would Baldwin get his hands on such information?" Lorne asked, shaking her head.

"The same way HQ did, I guess. Through the 'net."

"Really? Is nothing sacred anymore? I sometimes wonder if the 'net doesn't do more harm than good. I know it has its good side—I mean, for catching paedophiles and bringing them to justice—but in my book, the negatives far outweigh the positives."

"It's the superhighway, there to support good and bad info. That's something we all have to live with."

"I'll tell you what does stick in my throat with this list: I hate the way some of these countries plead poverty. For example China and South Korea, Taiwan—even Russia for that matter. From the images we see on TV, some people living in these countries live in mud houses, work in paddy fields for a dollar a day, their children dying from starvation; and all the time their governments are sitting pretty on all this gold. What's wrong with this world? Look at the last Olympics—you know, in Beijing—they tore down people's houses to build the stadiums needed for the games, even forcing some of the people whose houses had been destroyed to work on the construction sites, without proper equipment and clothing, for what? To add to their gold reserves?"

"All right, Lorne. Get off your soapbox." He smiled and picked up her list of questions. "So your Dad knows about you coming to France then?"

"Yeah. I rang him last night at the agreed time, while you were in the shower. He's not too happy about me being here, but he understands. He's looking after the dog for me."

"It's natural for him to be concerned." A sadness filled Tony's eyes, and he quickly looked down at the sheet in front of him again.

"Tony?"

"Going back to your list, I see that you do have some misgivings about the *capitaine*. You just weren't willing to share them with me, is that it?" He'd gone on the defensive, obviously realising she was going to ask something personal, and blocked the way.

Lorne shrugged, feeling awkward, and shuffled her feet under the table.

Tony asked, "How did Tom and Charlie take the news?"

She stared at the basket of surplus pastries on the table. "I don't know. I couldn't get hold of either one of them and ended up leaving a message on the machine." Her tear-filled eyes met his.

He surprised her by placing his hand on top of hers. "They'll understand, Lorne, and I'm sure you'll make things right with Charlie when you get home. Just take her back a nice outfit or something. I'm sure that'll suffice."

Her lip curled up. "And you think teenagers can be bought, just like that? You have a lot to learn, agent boy. It's obvious you've never been around kids."

Without answering, he rose from his chair. "Right, we better be going. You fit?" He headed out.

Clearly, she had unintentionally hit a nail that he didn't want to talk about on the head. Lorne swallowed, gathered the papers together, and ran out of the café after him. "Tony, I'm sorry."

"For what? Forget it, Lorne. I have."

Chapter Thirty

They trampled through sodden fields in the rain and crouched in the same place they'd used to stake out the chateau the day before.

"I don't know if you're aware, but they have a marvellous invention in the shops nowadays, Tony. It's called an umbrella. Ever heard of one?"

"Ssshhh!"

Lorne pulled her soaking wet T-shirt away from her shoulders and made a face behind his rain-soaked back.

The day had started out sunny and warm, but by mid-morning, dark clouds littered the sky, spitting out their contents and thoroughly drenching them. Nettles and brambles, which appeared to have multiplied overnight, surrounded them. Lorne watched the creepy crawlies darting around, seeking cover from the rain. *At least something around here has some sense.*

Because the autumn winds had stripped the leaves from the trees, the rain easily worked its way through the branches overhanging them, adding to Lorne's misery.

"Can you make out anything?"

"I think I can make out two lorries. There's a lot of activity going on over there, but we'll need to move in closer to get a better view." He stepped into the brambles in front of him, making Lorne wince. "That's better. Yep, two lorries."

"Is it the same scenario as yesterday?"

"Nope, one's loading, the other unloading. Jesus, there must be at least fifteen men over there."

"Can I take a look?" She shuffled up behind him. Resting her forearm on his back, she looked through the binoculars. "Oh shit!"

They heard a distant crash. Tony snatched back the glasses. "Hell. Can't see Baldwin being happy about that. One of the large ornate framed paintings has fallen off the back of the lorry—no pun intended—and crashed onto the drive."

A lot of shouting was heard and then silence. Lorne tugged impatiently at Tony's arm. "Come on. Give me a running commentary, for Christ's sake."

"Baldwin's just arrived. Wow! His face is darker than the clouds above us. He's pushing a few the blokes around. I get the impression no one is willing to own up to the mishap. Mind you, if I were in their shoes, I wouldn't either. Shit!"

Before Lorne had a chance to ask what had happened, a shot rang out. She covered her head with her hands.

"Fuck, he just shot one of his guys right between the eyes."

"Tony, *please*. Let's get out of here."

"No chance. Things are just hotting up. If we go now, that'll be another day wasted."

"But it's too dangerous—*he's* too dangerous—and if someone finds us, we'll be outnumbered."

"Don't be daft, Lorne. We're not going to be discovered. Have some faith in me, woman."

She mimicked his deep voice under her breath: "I've been doing this work for nearly twenty years, you know." But knowing he was an expert in his field did little to ease the fear growing and twisting her insides into knots.

"Jesus, Lorne, give it a rest." Tony kept a watchful eye on the events over at the chateau. "I thought the guys would back off after seeing one of their colleagues shot, but they're not. The shit's really hitting the fan. Even the drivers are getting caught up in the scuffle."

"Baldwin is well ticked off. He's waving his gun in their faces as if he was an SS officer during World War II, going from one to the other. Some of the guys are backing off, but most of them are standing their ground." Another shot interrupted Tony's commentary.

"I take it he's just shot another one?" Lorne asked, beginning to tremble.

* * *

"You no-good bunch of wankers. Anybody else want a go?"

Mario, one of the larger men, stepped forwards to challenge Baldwin.

"Come on then, Mario, if you think you're hard enough. You've been dying to have a crack at me ever since I wasted your shitty brother, anyway. Now's your chance, *boy*."

Mario leapt at Baldwin, but three men jumped on him to restrain him. Baldwin flinched and took an involuntary step back, wondering

118

if he had pushed the group too far that time. Shaking off the thought and determined to regain his authority, he approached Mario, almost touching noses with the man in an effort to intimidate him.

Mario sucked in a breath and spat in Baldwin's face. "Go on then, hard man. Shoot me; shoot all of us. And then what?"

Baldwin called the man's bluff and shot him twice in the head. Mario, who was built like a gorilla, crumpled to the ground, nearly taking the men who were holding him down with him. "Anyone else want to be a pathetic hero?"

Julio stepped forward, fear dancing in his eyes. "Boss, there'll be no more problems. I'll make sure of that."

"For once, Julio, you talk a lot of sense. Now, get these no-good shits back to work. Any more damage, and... Well, you know what'll happen." Baldwin waved the gun around before he left the group and marched back into the chateau.

* * *

"Fuck, he's just as callous as ever. That's three he's killed without even blinking. He's still a crazy bastard."

"Why?"

Tony shrugged, still watching the proceedings through the binoculars. "Because they challenged him."

"What's happening now?"

Tony shook his head. "Unbelievably, the men have picked up from where they left off. They dragged the three bodies onto the lawn and left them there as if they were sacks of rubbish."

"And Baldwin?"

"He went back into the house...chateau, whatever you want to call it."

"Look, Tony, I'm soaked to the skin here. How long before we leave?"

"Lightweight. Let's just give it half an hour and then I'll consider leaving."

Feeling miserable and fed up, she slumped back against the bank. A bramble dug her in the behind. She jumped forward. "Ouch! Fucking things stick to me like glue. How come they don't cut you up?"

"They probably know it wouldn't be wise to mess with me. Hey, hold on..."

"What?"

"One of the lorries is starting up, the one that was being loaded. Come on. We'll follow it."

Tony didn't wait for her to answer. He took off through the sodden field and headed for the car, with a drowned rat who vaguely resembled a former detective inspector close behind him. When they reached the car, they let the lorry pass and disappear round the first bend before Tony eased the car out of the lane and followed it, careful not to get too close.

"Where do you think it's heading? There's a port at Caen, isn't there?"

Tony vigorously shook his head. "No way is that lorry going anywhere near a ferry port. It would be far too risky. There's stolen art on board, remember."

"I know what cargo it's carrying, Tony. There's no need to treat me like an idiot."

"Sorry. My guess is it'll be going all the way to its final destination by road."

"We can't follow it, not all the way."

"Give me a chance, Lorne." He fetched his mobile from the glove compartment, punched in a number, and gave the details of the lorry—everything from its size, registration plate, and location— then asked for it to be tailed by satellite. Once the person at the other end gave him the all-clear, Tony dropped his speed and pulled into the nearest lay-by.

"Ah, the joys of being a spy," Lorne said sarcastically, feeling kind of foolish.

"It's a case of not what you know, but who you know, huh?" He smiled at her, winked, and tapped the side of his nose. "Let's head back to the hotel and wait for HQ to get back to us." After completing a three-point turn in the quiet road he headed back towards the chateau. "Get down!" Tony shouted. He placed a hand behind her neck and thrust her head into her lap.

Her nose thumped against her knee and made her eyes water. "Ouch! What the—?"

"Keep your head down. Pass me the see-through bag in the glove compartment, and then get down in the footwell."

She pulled out a bag with some kind of disguise in it and handed the items to him, one by one. He pulled on the flat cap before balancing the glasses on the edge of his nose, then he ripped off the backing of a fake moustache and stuck it to his top lip.

Despite the tension inside the car, Lorne found it hard not to laugh at the transformation. "Very fetching. All you need now is a string of onions and a bicycle. Do you mind telling me what's going on?"

"Ha bloody ha. Stay down there for the time being. As we came round the corner, I spotted two cars coming out of the chateau's drive. I'm going to tail them. I can't stay close without some form of disguise, can I?"

Lorne's damp clothes meant it didn't take long for her joints to cramp up. It worried her that she might not be able to sustain her position for long; they were at least twenty minutes from the nearest major town. She tried to keep the blood pumping through her legs by clenching and unclenching her muscles. "Can you make out who's in the cars?"

"Can't tell how many are in the front car, but the rear has four blokes in it, big fuckers too."

"Wonder what that's all about?"

"That's what we're about to find out."

Chapter Thirty-One

"Shit!" Tony swore as they approached the outskirts of Caen town centre.

"What?" Lorne bit down on her lip as the pain in her legs intensified.

"They've split up. I'm gonna stick with the front car." He dropped down a gear, and an impatient driver beeped his horn, but Tony just waved the driver past. "There are two people in the car, one burly bloke and one slightly smaller. I'm taking a gamble that the passenger is Baldwin. How you doing down there?"

"My legs feel like they belong to someone else. To be honest, I don't think I can stay like this for much longer." Lorne hated whining, but it happened to be the truth.

"Okay, you can sit back in your seat, provided you keep your head down. There's another car between us, so I doubt they'll be able to make out that I have a passenger on-board."

Settling back in the seat with her head tucked into her lap, Lorne mumbled, "Why thank you, master."

Tony started to mutter under his breath, ignoring her understandable grievance as he concentrated on keeping up with the car he thought was Baldwin's. The heavy traffic and frequent traffic lights tailing another car a difficult task. "I recognize this area. We're near Caen cathedral, and this road... Hmm... Interesting."

"What is?" Lorne inched her head up but lowered it quickly when Tony swiped it. "Ouch! You know, Tony, I wouldn't even treat my dog the way you're treating me right now."

"That's because you spoil your dog rotten. The car's stopped outside the hotel where we stayed with the *capitaine* and the *lieutenant*. Baldwin got out, and the driver sped off."

"Wow! That *is* interesting. What are we going to do now?"

"Sit and wait, girl. Sit and wait."

"Any chance we can 'sit and wait' in the café opposite the hotel?" Lorne remembered that they'd had a drink there the week before, where she'd had a hissy fit.

"I don't see why not. In fact, that's a great idea. Well done, Ms.

Simpkins."

"Patronising shit."

They ordered a baguette and a *café au lait* at the counter of the bustling café and sat at a table a few rows back from the window, an ideal position for surveillance purposes.

Then they waited. And waited. Dozens of people strolled in and out of the revolving door to the hotel, but not one piqued their interest. By nearly three o'clock, the customers in the café had dwindled. Only four of the thirty or so tables remained occupied.

A car pulled up outside the hotel, and a man hopped in the front. Voice hushed, Tony said, "It's him." He left a ten-euro note and a handful of centimes in the saucer with the bill. On the way out, he grabbed Lorne's hand, and they ran back to the car.

Tony tried to follow the car, but it was too late. By the time they pulled onto the main road, the traffic had built up, making it impossible to keep up with the other car. Tony slammed the heel of his hand into the steering wheel and cursed under his breath.

Lorne laid a reassuring hand on his forearm. "There'll be other times, don't worry."

"Yeah, I guess. If I dip into the hotel, will you drive around the block and pick me up in a few minutes?"

Lorne shot him a look and pointed at her chest. "Me, drive, around here? On the wrong side of the road, you mean?"

"It makes sense, Lorne. I'm the one wearing a disguise." He pulled the car over and jumped out, giving her little choice in the matter.

The more the cars beeped their horns at her, the more she broke out in sweat. *Damn you to hell, Tony.* If only she'd opened her mouth and told him she had a mini-phobia about driving strange cars, and her anxiety seemed worse than usual because their hire car had the controls on the opposite side to her own.

Her phobia had started at the age of nineteen. After passing her driving exam, she in her cockiness had taken her father's Cortina for a spin. Without his consent. An accident had occurred—though not caused by her—and the car had been a write-off. The guilt and terror of the incident usually reared its head when Lorne found herself in similar situations.

Her trembling hands gripped the steering wheel, and when she switched on the indicator, the wipers scraped on the windscreen instead. *Damn it!* Her nerves became even more on edge. Sucking in a few sharp breaths, she tried again, but as she pulled out into the traffic she forgot to put the car into gear and stalled it. *Jesus, Tony! Couldn't you have ordered an automatic?*

Hastily, she turned the key in the ignition, dipped the clutch, and selected first gear, all to a barrage of blasting horns. *Impatient frogs. Give me a bloody break, will you?* With the sweat pouring from her forehead and her hands still shaking, she eased into the traffic, breathing a huge sigh of relief when she turned into the side road on the left. Still in first gear, she crawled along the back of the hotel, and when she spotted the build-up ahead of her, panic rose again.

Seeing a free parking space, she pulled in and sat there with the engine still running. After taking a few seconds to calm her nerves, she drove off and attempted to filter into the stream of traffic at the end of the road. Five minutes later, someone finally signalled for her to pull out in front of him.

As she approached the hotel, she indicated. Once stopped, Lorne yanked on the handbrake, and darted into the passenger seat. Glancing up at Tony, she could tell by the thunderous look on his face he wasn't happy with how long it had taken her to return.

"What the—?" Tony opened the passenger door, but he stopped talking after one look at her terrified face. He ran past the front of the car and jumped into the driver's seat. Angry blasts surrounded them he waved an apology at a few and gave the finger to some of the more aggressive drivers passing by. "You all right, Lorne? What the hell happened?"

"Don't ever do that to me again." Her voice trembled, matching her hands, which were stuffed into her lap.

"Do what?"

"Please, can we just get out of here, Tony?"

Out of the corner of her eye she saw him shrug and heard him let out a frustrated sigh. As he pulled into the traffic and headed back to their hotel, Lorne's panic soon subsided.

Back in their hotel room, Tony threw the car keys on the bedside table between the two beds. "So?"

Her eyes narrowed and met his. Shrugging, she replied, "So?"

Sighing, Tony flopped onto his bed. "You first. What happened back there?"

Lorne shook her head. She felt foolish for panicking. "Nothing happened back there. I can't stand traffic, that's all." She looked at the floor to avoid his eyes and tried to change the subject. "What did you find out at the hotel?"

"Nothing. For a start, they didn't understand what I was getting at—or so they said—and for another, I don't think they would have told me anything anyway. The girl was snooty and uncooperative."

"Did you see anyone hanging around?"

"Nope…" Just then, Tony's phone rang. Placing a finger to his lips, he walked over to the dressing table where his notepad was. He flipped it open to a blank page and took notes, making the odd grunting noise as he listened to the caller. All of a sudden, he turned to face her, and his eyes widened as he motioned for her to come over to him.

Alarmed, she shot off the bed and looked down at the pad, but his writing proved to be an unreadable scrawl.

She shrugged and mouthed, "I can't read it."

He tutted and wrote in capital letters, *GET YOUR BAGS PACKED. WE'RE ON THE MOVE.*

Lorne ran into the bathroom and quickly threw all her toiletries in her bag and stepped back into the bedroom just as Tony hung up.

"What's going on?"

"HQ told me it looks like they're on the move up at the chateau. They're loading up a number of cars."

Within minutes, they'd both packed their bags. Tony settled the guesthouse bill, and they were on their way back to the chateau.

Chapter Thirty-Two

They raced back to the chateau and hid in their usual spot, but Lorne soon realised that they needn't have bothered. The chateau and its surroundings lay silent, free from movement of any description. During the half-hour ride, it looked like everyone had cleared out.

Tony contacted Headquarters when it was clear what had happened. "What's going on? Any idea when they left?" After a brief pause, a worried expression crossed his face and quickly disappeared. "We'll make our way back to the car. Send the route to me via my phone, will you? Okay, be in touch soon."

Lorne ran after him, and they were in the car before either of them spoke again, "Well?"

"They've all shipped out, by the looks of it."

"How do your guys know that? I thought they were tracking the truck."

Tony laughed. "We're not dealing with bobbies here, Lorne. Yes, HQ was keeping an eye on the truck, but we have more than one satellite, you know. MI6 don't need to be told what to do every step of the way. They knew we wouldn't be able to observe the chateau 24/7, so they've been observing it for us—well, after I made the call, that is."

Crossing her arms across her chest, Lorne stared at the road ahead, feeling as if he'd spoken to her like a child. "I was just fucking asking. No need to treat me like a bloody idiot," she snapped.

He patted her thigh. "Sorry, Lorne. Forgot how sensitive you are at the moment."

His patronising incensed her even more, and had it not been for his phone indicating a message, she would have lashed out. *Saved by the bell, jerk!*

"According to HQ, the last vehicle left about twenty minutes ago."

Forgetting about their little spat, Lorne sat up and turned to face him. "How many vehicles, and are they all travelling in the same direction?"

He smirked and nodded. "There are five vehicles, two lorries and three cars. At the moment, they're all going in the same direction. Will you get the map out of the glove compartment?"

Lorne pulled out the map they'd bought a few days before and opened it. Tony handed her his phone, which showed a map of where the vehicles had been last located. She transferred the information to the map on her knees.

"Come on, then, Ms ex-DI. Where do you think they're heading?"

It took Lorne precisely two minutes to work it out. She tapped the N158 on the map with her index finger. "Knowing Baldwin as we do, I'd hazard a guess he's taking the road that leads down south." She followed the road and tapped the town she thought would be their next probable stop. "My powers of deduction say Le Mans. It conjures up images of the rich and famous—it does to me, anyway."

She glanced sideways and saw Tony nodding, looking impressed. "Well, there's only one way to find out." He pressed his foot to the floor, and the car shot forward. "You keep hold of my phone. They'll send another message if Baldwin and his motley crew change direction."

Lorne hunted through her handbag, pulled out a black notebook and pen, and made notes while Tony concentrated on tracking down the escaping pack of vehicles.

Before long the light had faded, and as darkness surrounded them, they saw a signpost telling them Le Mans was sixty kilometres ahead. With the smooth, constant rhythm of the car travelling on the virtually clear road, Lorne almost dropped off to sleep several times. Her neck started to throb from her head dipping backwards and forwards.

Tony spoke. "If we're going to stop in Le Mans, it'll take us approximately forty minutes to get there. Why don't you take a quick nap?"

"What if a message comes through?" she asked, stifling a yawn.

"I'll deal with it." Tony held out his hand for the phone.

She placed the phone in his outstretched hand, folded up the map, and slid down in her seat.

Almost forty-five minutes later, Lorne woke with a start when she realised the car had stopped. "Are we here?" She stretched and put her hand over her mouth as she yawned.

"Yes, sleepyhead."

"Are they around?"

Tony nodded towards the Anjou Hotel opposite them. "We can't stay there though, and I can't see another hotel or guest house around here."

"What do you suggest, then? That we sleep in the car?"

"Would you have a problem with that?"

Thinking she could hardly say yes after just waking up from a quick doze, Lorne shook her head.

Tony laughed. "As if I'd let you spend the night in a car. I'm not that heartless, Lorne. I've contacted HQ, and they've managed to book us into a small hotel around the corner. They're going to keep an eye on the vehicles overnight and ring us if they move on."

Within ten minutes, they had located the hotel and were settled in their room. Glancing at the only bed—a double—Lorne couldn't help feeling a little uncomfortable. There wasn't even a sofa where one of them could spend the night. She didn't have the courage to tell Tony how awkward she felt, so she trotted off to the bathroom to get changed.

She came back out and shot under the covers, embarrassed to be seen in her pink pyjamas.

He smiled. "Everything all right?"

Lorne poked her head out from under the quilt, nodded, and turned to face the other way. A few minutes later, the bed dipped, and Tony got in behind her. Clinging to the edge of the bed, she feared what might happen if she relaxed and bumped into him. The bed shifted again when he reached over to switch off the bedside light.

Silence.

As she listened to the change in his breathing, Lorne gently turned to face Tony. From the light filtering through the thin curtains, she studied the outline of his strong, handsome yet scarred face, and something stirred within her. Her eyes were drawn to his lips, and she imagined them roaming the length and breadth of her body...

"Are you watching me, Lorne?"

She gasped, and her cheeks warmed. She was thankful of the dim darkness surrounding them. "Um... No... It's just that I prefer to sleep facing this way. I usually spend the night cuddling my collie, if you must know." *Why in God's name did you tell him that?*

Lorne saw his teeth show in the dark and knew he'd found her explanation amusing. She wanted to bite her tongue off for the way it had run away from her.

He mumbled something under his breath and laughed softly.

"Was that intended for me to hear or not?" She puffed up her pillow and leaned against the headboard, tucking her arms around her knees, another show of defiance she'd often used during her ill-fated marriage. *Men, you always have an answer for everything, always need to get that final word in, don't you?*

Tony turned on the lamp beside him and mimicked her position. "Oh, Lorne, your sense of humour really has gone AWOL, hasn't it?"

She wasn't sure what she had expected him to say, but it wasn't that. She also hadn't expected him to speak so quietly. It was the complete opposite of how she had anticipated the conversation progressing. Silent tears ran down her hot cheeks, and staring at the wall in front of her, she shrugged.

"Look, I know the past year has been tough on you, but you need to dig deep for your resolve. Life goes on. *Your* life goes on, with or without those you've lost. It has to. Think of it like this: If you insist on letting it eat away at you, you're letting down those who lost their lives."

She let his words sink in for a few moments. He was right, and suddenly she felt foolish, not for the first time on their trip. She turned to face him. Their gazes locked. "Is that what happened to you, Tony?" she whispered.

Something flashed in his eyes, making her think she had touched a nerve. For a minute, he sat silent, staring at the wall in front of him. She pushed down the panic rising within. The last thing she wanted to do was alienate him, a man she knew very little about. All she knew was that he was regarded as one of the top agents in the UK, who in order to gain his current status had probably put his personal life on hold.

He sucked in a deep breath and let it out slowly. "Her name was Miranda." His hands raked through his short hair, and Lorne placed a comforting hand on his forearm, to encourage him to go on. "We lived together for a while. At first, she found my work exciting, every time I came back from an assignment, the first thing she wanted to know was the whys and wherefores of where I had been, *et cetera*. As you know, we're not allowed to divulge that sort of thing…"

"So what did you do?"

He took another breath. His face twisted with guilt. "I had to be resourceful, come up with imaginative stories to keep her happy. Sometimes, I'd catch a headline bulletin on the news and instantly make up an intriguing story that sounded plausible, just to satisfy her interest. Most of them were so far from the truth it was laughable."

"But why? I mean, most—no, all—relationships should be built on trust…"

"I know they should be, but…"

Silence, again.

Lorne soon figured out what he was getting at. "Sex. You mean the more creative your stories were, the greater your sex life became."

He shot her a look that said her analogy was correct. "Don't think badly of me, Lorne. It's what men do. We want our ladies to think of us as real heroes."

She shook her head.

"What?"

"When it comes down to it, you men really don't understand us women at all."

"Okay, maybe not in your case. After all, the roles were reversed for you and Tom, weren't they? You were perceived to be the heroine in your relationship. Didn't your job get in the way, come the end?"

He had a point. Her career had driven several nails into the marriage coffin during their turbulent fourteen years together. "Okay, you got me there. Come the end, as you put it, Tom rebelled against the job, and eventually me, but we're not talking about me. Was this Miranda high-maintenance?"

He laughed then fell silent again. "Daddy was very rich. She wanted for nothing. When she moved into my one-bed apartment in London, it was a bit of a let-down for her. The minute she stepped through the door and I saw the way her face dropped, I knew I had to pull out all the stops to make her happy."

"So you thought lying to her would keep her happy?"

"It did to begin with. Even during sex, she wanted to know about what torture techniques I used to obtain information."

"You're kidding! Why didn't you just dump her? I mean, if you knew the minute she stepped into your apartment that it would be hard to impress her…"

"I was in love with her."

"Are you sure it was love and not lust? I know you men always think with that thing dangling between your legs, but really. What colour eyes did she have?"

"What?"

"You heard me. What colour eyes did she have?"

"Brown, I think."

"There you go. You've just proved my point. If you really loved her, you would've shot the answer back at me without needing to stall for thinking time. And then to give an answer you're unsure of..."

"Smartarse bitch. You think you have all the answers, don't you?"

"Most of the time, yes. Go on with your story. What happened to end the relationship."

Tony chewed on a fingernail and then expelled another deep breath. "She came home one day—correct that, she staggered home drunk one day. I wasn't too happy to see her in such a state. She'd been out with the girls and blabbed."

He fell silent again, and Lorne prompted him to finish. "And?"

"One of the girls she'd blabbed to, her father happens to be high up in the government. Word got back to my boss about a few of the tall stories I'd told, and I was hauled over the coals about it. My boss ordered me to dump her as she couldn't be trusted. I tried to tell them I would never divulge secrets about the job and that I'd made up the stories, but they wouldn't listen. The subject was closed. Either I dumped her, or the service dumped me, end of."

"Crikey. So...?"

"That night I went home, packed her bags, and waited for her to come home. I told her we were finished and that I was taking her home to Daddy. I'll never forget the look on her face. If I didn't know any better, I'd say she felt relieved. Of course, she didn't say it. She pouted a lot and asked me to reconsider. Deep down, I could tell she wanted out."

"Do you think what she did was intentional?"

"Divulging my imaginary assignments, you mean?"

Lorne nodded, feeling sorry for him. He'd obviously never been in a loving relationship before and therefore mistook Miranda's attention for something it clearly wasn't.

"I'm not sure, I've always had a nagging doubt, but..."

"Do you know where she is now?"

"Yeah. Six months after she left me, she married an up-and-coming MP."

"Sounds to me like you had a lucky escape."

"Why, thank you, counsellor."

"Hey, there's someone out there for you, Tony…" She turned to him and was surprised to see his eyes glistening. Without thinking about what she was doing, she reached over and pecked him on the cheek, then laid her head on his bare chest. He tensed up for a moment, and then his breathing returned to normal, which caused the coarse hairs on his chest to tickle her face and neck.

His arm lazily came to rest on her back, and a sigh escaped her lips. It felt good to be in a man's arms again after such a long time. The *capitaine* encounter had been pure lust on her part, nothing compared to how she was feeling now. Something stirred inside as his hand brushed lightly over her back.

Lorne's phone rang. She shot up and grabbed her bag. Her father's number showed up on the display, making her worry. "Hello?"

"Thank God. You're all right. It's half past nine, Lorne."

"Oh flippin' heck… I'm sorry, Dad. We've had a hell of a day." *Shouldn't have said that.* She cursed the way the words had slipped out so easily.

"Oh? Is everything all right?"

"It's fine, Dad. Didn't mean to worry you. We're on the move…" Tony tapped her arm. She faced him, and he shook his head.

"Lorne? Lorne… What do you mean, you're on the move?"

"Sorry, but I think I've said enough already."

"Enough? I think you'll find the opposite, young lady. Now, what in God's name is going on?"

She hated lying to her father, and her heart pounded, but by the glare Tony was giving her, she knew she didn't have a choice in the matter. "Sorry, Dad, didn't mean to mislead you. What I meant was, we had to change hotels. They had double booked our rooms." She could tell by the tone in her father's voice that he didn't believe her, and the call lasted for only another few minutes. "Sorry again, Dad, for missing the nine o'clock deadline. It won't happen again."

With the underlying feeling she'd upset her father, Lorne turned her back on Tony and settled in to try to sleep. Luckily, he didn't force the issue, and she lay awake for hours listening to him breathe.

Chapter Thirty-Three

Lorne awoke in a daze, and to her horror, she found herself sprawled out on Tony's side of the bed, with him nowhere to be seen. A strange noise made her sit up quickly. It took her a few seconds to work out that the sound was Tony's phone vibrating its way across the console table.

"Tony?" No response. She called out again as she threw back the covers. She put her ear to the bathroom door and heard the shower running. He probably couldn't hear her calling him. *Shit! Do I answer his phone or what?*

Lorne picked up his mobile, knocked on the door, and burst into the bathroom, eyes tightly shut. "Sorry, Tony…but your phone is ringing."

The shower curtain rustled, and the rings slid back on the rail. Water dripped on her outstretched hand as the phone left her palm. Lorne stepped back into the bedroom, closing the door behind her.

Within seconds, Tony burst in. "Shit. Get dressed. They're on the move again."

"What? When?"

"Just get dressed, Lorne. Sorry, you don't have time for a shower. You've got two minutes."

Lorne sprinted back and forth between the bathroom and the bedroom, gathering her things together. They were packed and ready to set off in exactly one minute and fifty-five seconds.

As soon as they had settled into the car, Lorne demanded to know what was going on.

"HQ told me the vehicles have split up…"

She turned to him, disappointment written on her face. "Great. What do we do now?"

"I'm not concerned about the two lorries. I was expecting them to take a different route to Baldwin anyway, but if we can't find him…then we're up the proverbial."

They pulled up outside the hotel where Baldwin and his men had stayed the previous night and were stunned by the thick crowd of people blocking the street.

Puzzled, Tony rang HQ to see if they could shed any light on anything. "I see… Well that's fucking fantastic, isn't it? How many days? The bastard must've known about this." He ended the call and thumped the steering wheel.

"What?"

"Looks like we've hit town at the wrong time."

"Meaning?"

"The Le Mans bike rally is about to start. It's one of the biggest events staged in the area at this time of the year."

"And, you think Baldwin knew about this?"

"Don't you?" he snapped back.

The crinkles on Tony's forehead showed how annoyed he was. Lorne decided to let him cool down before attempting to speak again. She watched the crowds jostling in the street in front of and around them, and she struggled to fight back the sinking feeling that threatened to spoil her day.

Tony broke the silence first. "Sorry."

She shot him a puzzled look. "What for?"

"For snapping. For dragging you out here for a second time… For involving you in the first place…"

"Stop it. We've hit a minor hiccup, that's all. He'll emerge somewhere soon, and when he does, we'll be on his trail again." She had no idea if her words had any merit or not, but Tony nodded, shrugged, and started up the car.

"You know what, Ms ex-DI? You talk a lot of sense. How about we grab some breakfast?"

Enjoying the brief role reversal of keeping Tony buoyant and motivated, she smiled. "Sounds like a brilliant idea, and it'll give your guys a chance to try to locate some of the vehicles."

He returned her smile and patted her leg. Lorne took the gesture to mean, "Thanks for keeping me on the straight and narrow." It made her ponder if they were actually turning into a good team.

They found a local café. Neither of them were hungry in the end, but they settled at a table with a *café au lait* each.

It was a full two hours before London contacted them again. Tony snatched his phone off the table the second it rang. "Yep… Bloody brilliant, any suggestions?… Right. Get back to me ASAP."

"By the look on your face, I'd say things haven't exactly gone according to plan, back there."

"You could say that. They don't have a clue where Baldwin or his men are."

"So, what do you think we should do?"

"I was wondering whether I should pose as an associate of Baldwin's and try to get some info out of the receptionist at the hotel. Maybe someone picked up where they were heading or something."

Lorne shook her head, knowing how unlikely the scenario was, but then she had second thoughts and shrugged. "I guess we don't have any other decent alternatives springing to mind."

They headed back to the car. Tony edged the car through the crowds, who by now were spilling into the roads, not caring if they got knocked down. He pulled up outside the hotel, and left the engine running as he ran up the steps into reception.

Lorne took the map from the glove compartment and studied it. *If I was Baldwin, what would I do? Which way would I go?* They had already come to the conclusion his ultimate destination was likely to be his yacht. All they needed now would be to figure out his probable route.

Come on, girl. Get back into police mode—better still, get back to devious thinking, Unicorn thinking! If I was him, I'd utilise this commotion to my advantage, but how?

She glanced at the map again. The trouble was, they had followed three cars, and London didn't have a clue where any of them were at that moment. Even if London did find the cars, they didn't know which of those cars Baldwin travelled in.

Lorne trailed the map with her finger to the nearest town, Bourges. She looked at the scale in the corner and worked out the approximate distance. *Two and a half hours away.* But something gnawed at her insides. She had an inkling the criminal was still in the vicinity, using the disruption around them to his advantage. *Come on, London. Give us something to go on, please!*

The car door opened sharply, startling Lorne. Relief swept through her when Tony jumped into the driver's seat. "Well, that was a waste of time," he said. "No one spoke English, and I struggled to make them understand what I was getting at, let alone who I was talking about. I didn't know if he was booked in as Baldwin or what." He nodded at the map. "Any thoughts?"

"Some."

"Care to share them with me?" he asked, amused that she appeared to be distracted.

Lorne shook her head. "Sorry. I was miles away." She turned to look at him and saw devilment lingering in his eyes. She frowned. "What's that look for?"

His mouth turned up and made her heart pound faster in her chest. Her cheeks warmed, and she switched her focus from Tony to the crowd outside.

"Nothing. I was just thinking about what would have happened in bed last night if your father hadn't rung."

Still avoiding his gaze, she swallowed noisily. "Shouldn't we be considering the future—I mean, what our next move should be?"

He laughed, obviously enjoying her embarrassment. She could do little to stop the hairs on the back of her neck standing on end. *Stay focused on Baldwin, Lorne,* she warned herself as she turned to look at him. Their gazes locked, and Tony leaned towards her and pressed his lips gently against hers. Surprised, she shivered as an electric current shot between them.

Tony must have felt it too, for he pulled away and wiped the back of his hand across his mouth.

Lorne cleared her throat and joked, "You rubbing it in or trying to remove it?"

His eyes bore into hers, and she thought she could see hunger burning deep inside. "I'm sorry," he replied quietly.

She shook her head. "For what, kissing me?"

"Yes, I shouldn't have done it."

Lorne gazed through the windscreen and mumbled, "Don't be sorry. I enjoyed it."

Then she spotted something else that set her pulse racing. *Baldwin!* She pointed a shaking finger out the window. "Tony, look!"

He tried to peer through the thick crowd. "What?! I can't see a damn thing. You'll have to tell me."

"I'm sure I just saw Baldwin."

"You're kidding. Where?"

"A man in a black suit came out of that building over there. Is it a bank? He got into a waiting car. I'm sure it was him. Hurry!"

Tony eased the car through a gap in the crowd, and it didn't take him long to pick up the tail of the vehicle. Fifty feet in front of them, going at a snail's pace due to the milling crowd, was a black Lexus that appeared to be heading towards a blue sign up ahead, a French motorway sign.

"Quick, Tony. He's getting away."

"Are you positive it was him? Because if that car is heading for the motorway, there will be no turning back if we're wrong, not for miles."

"Then you're going to have to take my word for it. I'm ninety per cent sure it was him."

"That'll do for me." Tony revved the engine to try to disperse the crowd. His persistence paid off, and as the crowd thinned out Lorne saw the Lexus join the motorway, and Tony followed.

Chapter Thirty-Four

After travelling non-stop for almost two-and-a-half hours, it soon became apparent that Lorne's guess had been right. Bourges would be their next stop.

Tony kept their hired Renault close behind the powerful Lexus, whilst still making sure that there were at least three or four cars between them and Baldwin. Tony commented that the Lexus didn't seem to be in any kind of hurry to get to its location, which was fine by them.

Lorne was deep in thought about the kiss they'd shared, which neither had mentioned since. She jumped when Tony spoke, pulling her back from her wandering thoughts.

"Here we go. Looks like you were right."

The Lexus pulled off the motorway and onto the slip road signposted for Bourges. Tony dropped his speed when the cars between them carried on up the A71 motorway, leaving them directly behind Baldwin. Lorne opened the glove compartment, took out the disguise, and handed it to him.

"We better add 'mind reader' to your list of abilities."

Lorne laughed. "I didn't realise there was a list going. We'll chat about that later. I'm dying to hear what else is on it."

They followed the Lexus into town on the N151, going past the small airfield on the right. They saw the sign for a German cemetery. An image of the day Lorne spent with the *capitaine* sprang to her mind, and she quickly discarded it. That was something she definitely didn't need reminding about, especially with the way things were developing with Tony.

The Lexus pulled up outside the stunning Best Western Hotel, and out stepped Baldwin. He stretched and patted the roof of the car for the driver to move on before he entered the hotel.

"Jesus, I never thought I'd say these words," said Tony as he drove past, "but boy, am I glad to see Baldwin." He blew out a relieved sigh. "We took a risk following the Lexus, and thanks to you, our gamble has paid off." Fifty yards up the road, he brought the car to a halt and they both swivelled in their seats to look behind.

"What do we do now?"

"Now that we've sighted Baldwin, I'll get in touch with London and get them to keep an eye on his car. I just saw it pull into the hotel's car park. We'll hang around here for a while, make sure Baldwin stays inside; then we'll need to find a hotel close by with vacancies."

"Why don't I go find us some lunch?"

Tony fished out his wallet from his jacket pocket, handed her a ten-euro note, and gave her a crooked smile. "Please, try to find something different. I'm all baguetted out."

"I'll do my best, but baguettes appear to be the Frenchies' staple diet. I'll try to find a hotel, too."

Tony nodded and brushed his lips against hers, surprising her again. "Be careful, keep your wits about you, and don't be long, just in case Baldwin does take off somewhere."

Lorne set off and soon stumbled across a Patisserie that sold proper sandwiches as well as the dreaded baguette. She bought a ham and cheese, a tuna mayo sandwich, and a few almond croissants that took her fancy. She left the baker's, turned right, and spotted a small hotel squeezed in the middle of a row of shops. Nothing as high-class as Baldwin's choice, but she knew it would likely suit her and Tony's needs as long as it had a shower and a bed that would do for them.

She crossed the road and booked a room before heading back to Tony. She plonked herself back in the passenger seat, feeling pleased with what she'd achieved in the ten minutes she'd been gone. But as she offered Tony the two bags containing his lunch, Lorne noticed his eyes had widened, and his jaw had dropped open. "It's not that surprising, you know. They do have normal bread here too in France..."

He halted her with his hand and shook his head. "You'll never guess who I've just seen going into Baldwin's hotel."

Considering the population of France, Lorne found it almost impossible to guess, but looking at the disbelief on Tony's face, she knew she wasn't going to like his answer. "Come on, Tony. The suspense is killing me."

"Renée."

Lorne's brow furrowed, and Tony bit back, "Jesus, your detective brain really has gone rusty, hasn't it?"

Hurt by his put-down, she snapped, 'Well? Tell me then, smartarse. Stop bloody playing games."

"Okay, I'll spell it out for you: Lieutenant Renée Levelle."

"*What*?!'

"You heard me. Renée just entered *his* hotel."

"Jesus! By herself?"

"Looked like it. So maybe your *capitaine* wasn't the problem after all."

"Bugger off, Tony. He was never 'my' *capitaine*, anyway. I told you that you were wrong about him, but you wouldn't listen. Don't forget…" She paused as the picture of the one she'd loved passed before her mind's eye. "The *capitaine* was one of Jacques' closest friends."

Tony eyed her suspiciously and took his time to respond. "Hmm…"

"Is that it? Is that the best you can offer, *agent boy?*"

A heavy silence filled the car. They both twisted in their seats, eyeing the hotel behind them.

Lorne broke through the deafening silence first. "So, what happens now?"

"It's simple… We wait."

She could tell his annoyance still lingered and tried to lighten the mood. "We could always eat lunch. I didn't get a baguette, as ordered." Smiling, she offered him the two bags again. That time he took them, if a little hesitantly. "Will ham and cheese be all right?"

"Whatever. I'd prefer it if it was washed down with a nice pint of Bitter."

Lorne let out the breath she'd been holding in as the tension lightened in the car. "Huh, some hope of that happening over here. Do you think they even know what Bitter is?"

Tony shrugged, turned in his seat and angled the rear-view mirror towards the hotel's entrance before tucking into his sandwich, giving the impression it was the first time he'd eaten in two weeks.

Deep in thought, Lorne nibbled at her tuna sandwich, her mind shooting off in different directions, going over all that had happened to them in the past twenty-four hours. Everything, from nearly making love to Tony, to the shock of learning that the *lieutenant* was probably tucked up in a hotel room with Baldwin.

"Penny for them?" Tony asked, through a mouthful of bread.

Her head shook slowly and took to people-watching the neatly turned-out French ladies in their couture skirt suits, window shopping in their lunch hours. Tony kept a vigilant eye trained on the rear-view mirror.

About an hour or so later Tony announced, "Shit... There's Baldwin."

Just as Baldwin crossed the road, Lorne turned in her seat and watched as he climbed into the same Lexus. "Did Renée come out of the hotel before him then?"

"Didn't see her... I don't like the look of this."

"What do you mean?"

His features etched with concern, Tony planted a kiss on her lips.

"What the hell... Why did you do that?"

He pointed in front of him, and she noticed the Lexus a few cars ahead of them. "Oh, I see. Where do you think he's heading now?"

"I haven't got a clue. I'll get onto London ask them to pick up his tail." He made the call. After he hung up, he said, "I'm going in."

"What? Into the hotel, you mean? What if Baldwin comes back?"

"It's a risk I'm willing to take, Lorne. Something doesn't feel right, and until I put that feeling to bed it's going to be a distraction. I'll be right back."

Before she could argue, he'd leapt out of the car. She looked over her shoulder and watched him run into the hotel.

* * *

That receptionist proved to be more helpful, saying that Baldwin had just vacated his room. Tony pretended that he was an associate of the criminal and that Baldwin had thought he'd left something behind in his room. The receptionist rang for the bellboy, who showed him up to the suite recently vacated by Baldwin.

The bellboy unlocked the door and threw it open. His face went ashen, and he stumbled back into the hallway.

Tony barged into the room and immediately told the dumbfounded young man to "Call the police!"

He heard the bellboy's feet thunder away in the hallway behind him as he tentatively walked towards the bed, where he saw the naked body of Lieutenant Renée Levelle lying on the bed.

Actually, she wasn't entirely naked. A sheet of hotel-headed notepaper lay across her breast. On it, in capital letters, were the words, *LORNE IS NEXT.*

"Bastard." Tony searched the room quickly, to see if he could find any possible clues as to where Baldwin would turn up next. He found nothing in the lavish suite, not that he'd thought he would. He left the room before the locals turned up, suspecting he would be held for questioning, despite discovering the *lieutenant*'s body with the bellboy.

Instead of taking the lift, he found the access to the stairs and ran down. He paused at the bottom, to make sure no one could see him trying to sneak out. The receptionist, who was dealing with a guest, turned her back. Tony took his opportunity and bolted out of the hotel.

"Phew, that was a close shave." he said as he settled behind the steering wheel. "Lorne?"

But he was talking to himself. Lorne was nowhere to be seen.

Chapter Thirty-Five

Lorne struggled. "Get off me, you…you disgusting piece of—"

Baldwin slapped her across her face. "So, Ms ex-Detective, we meet at last. Yes, I can see the resemblance with dear Charlie, now—and I don't mean just a physical similarity, either. It is clear whose side of the family she gets her feistiness from."

Baldwin laughed, and a chill raced along Lorne's spine. One hand covered her stinging cheek while the other lay in her lap, clenched into a tight fist, ready to strike out. *Why the hell did I let my guard down? How in God's name did I allow myself to get abducted?*

She could have kicked herself for not paying attention to her surroundings. She truly was rusty. Baldwin had sent one of his men to snatch her, and he dragged her from the car, screaming and shouting. To her dismay, not *one* person attempted to help her. The brute threw her into the back of the Lexus, where she came face-to-face with the sadistic maniac who, over the years, had successfully ripped both her professional and personal lives to shreds.

"You won't get away with this, Baldwin."

The two men in the front seats laughed, but the Unicorn sitting alongside her did nothing.

Slyly glancing out of the corner of her eye, Lorne could see his head was turned towards her, a smug grin pulling at his mouth. She swallowed noisily. "Tony won't let anything happen to me… London HQ have been tracking your vehicle…"

His fist connected with her face, hard. She instinctively sent her hands up to cover her nose and mouth. She fought hard not to cry, to show any weakness, but failed miserably. She didn't need a doctor to tell her that he had broken her nose. Remembering she had placed a serviette in her pocket from when she'd eaten her sandwich, she took it out and dabbed at her nostrils.

"Right. Let's get one thing straight: You speak *only* when you're spoken to. Have you got that?"

She turned to face him, her eyes brimming with tears.

When she didn't respond, Baldwin raised his fist towards her face again and stopped within inches of her left eye. "I said… Have you got that?"

Lorne felt paralysed with fear for the first time in her life. She thought quickly knowing her survival would be down to the training she had received in the Met, with 'how to manage criminals' top of the list. An image of her daughter popped into her head. *If Charlie managed to survive his brutality, there's no reason why I can't do the same.* She nodded, and his clenched fist dropped to the seat between them.

"As long as you understand that, Lorne, there's no reason for us not to get along. You and I could become…good friends," he said in what he clearly thought was a seductive manner. His two henchmen chuckled, and Baldwin's hand unclenched to stroke its way from her knee up to her thigh. Lorne squeezed her eyes shut and stiffened beneath his touch. He laughed, and Lorne suspected she was in for an uncomfortable ride, in more ways than one.

How the hell can I get out of this? What a mess, girl—what a bloody mess!

The white serviette had already changed colour from soaking up her blood, and Baldwin surprised her, taking a packet of tissues out of the pocket on the car door and handing them to her. "Not for your benefit, but mine. I don't want you bleeding all over my leather seats." His laugh chilled her to the bone.

Lorne stuffed the used serviette back in her jacket pocket, tore open the tissues, and continued to mop up the blood still pouring from her nose. After a while, the blood loss made her feel light-headed, and the smell of the leather interior made her want to throw up. But the fear of what Baldwin would do to her if she vomited forced her to swallow down the bile forming in her throat.

"Now, tell me what you and that cretin of an agent know?"

"We know nothing," she snapped, immediately regretting her harsh words.

"Want another thump?"

Lorne shuffled backwards until she was up against the door, Baldwin's arm shot out and grabbed her by the wrist. Twisting her arm, he forced her back beside him.

"Play nicely, and you'll come out of this smelling of roses. Don't, and you'll come out of this resembling a pit bull who lost a fight. Do you know what happens to pit bulls that lose, Lorne?"

Petrified, she shook her head.

He placed a pointed finger to her temple and his mouth towards her ear. He shouted, "*Bang!*"

Lorne flinched and let out a muffled scream. Despite trying her hardest to remain calm and unperturbed her nerves were already shattering.

"Now, tell me what you know?"

I have to tell him some of it. "Okay, we don't know much." Lorne swallowed more bile. It combined with the blood at the back of her throat, making it a struggle for her to talk, but the thought of his fist connecting with her face again urged her on. "We know that you're involved in stealing art," she paused, waiting for him to speak. When he didn't, she sighed heavily. "And it's pretty obvious you're receiving a lot of help from the police in this country…"

"Go on. Don't stop there. This is just getting interesting."

"That's about it… We saw the *lieutenant* go into your hotel, presumably for a…rendezvous with you." She eyed him out the corner of her eye and noticed a smile had crept onto his lips. *Huh! He's not even going to deny it, the crazy shit!*

"That's pretty good for an ex-copper. And you're right. I did get some help from the police and Interpol in the form of Renée, but not anymore…"

Lorne refused to give Baldwin the satisfaction of a reaction to his unfinished sentence. When she remained quiet, her abductor finished his story.

"What, no twenty questions, Lorne? You disappoint me, or maybe the broken nose I gave you has helped to finally keep you in line." He paused to laugh, and Lorne shuddered despite, trying to hold back the threatening nausea. "Let's just say the sexy French *lieutenant* has outlived her usefulness."

Lorne sucked in a breath. She ended up having a coughing fit as she choked on the blood and bile caught in her throat. *How could he?* But she already knew the answer to that, and again, she feared for her own safety. Which led her to fear she'd never see her family again.

Dad. If I don't call before nine this evening, he'll send out reinforcements.

Don't be an idiot, Lorne. Tony will have that all in hand by now. As soon as he realises you're missing, he'll get on to London, and… The conversation went on in her mind as different likely scenarios played out.

She saw Baldwin smile. "I can see your tiny copper brain working overtime, ex-Inspector, but I'd advise you not to go there. I pull the strings, remember, and if I decide to leave you dangling, there is little you and your so-called rescuers, can do about it."

Lorne stared at the passing countryside and refused to answer. She squinted as she wracked her brain for ideas to help her escape; at the same time, she prayed neither Tony nor London would let her down.

Chapter Thirty-Six

After telling Headquarters about the two mishaps that had occurred, Tony was ordered to pursue Baldwin. London had already informed him they had picked up the Lexus and were following it via satellite. Pulling out into a gap in the traffic, he immediately ground to a halt when someone bashed into him. Distracted thinking about Renée and Lorne, he hadn't seen the car coming out of the side turn.

"What the fu—you bloody imbecile."

Since driving in France, he'd already come to the conclusion the average French resident couldn't drive properly, so he wasn't surprised when one of them hit him. But he was bloody annoyed about it. He feared by the time the police turned up and took the relevant statements, Lorne would be miles away. As the irate Frenchman stood in the road, gesticulating furiously at him, Tony rang London again and apprised them of his latest balls-up.

Headquarters assured him that they would keep an eye on Baldwin's progress and that he should get the situation he was now caught up in sorted out ASAP.

Tony stepped out of the car and into a crowd of fuming locals, who had clearly taken the elderly Frenchman's side, despite the old man ramming *him* in the side. The far-off sirens made him wonder if the police were coming to attend to the dead lieutenant, or the fracas now surrounding him. Either way, he got more pissed off by the minute and promised himself he'd never step foot in Bourges again.

The situation was turning out to be so farcical, the thought crossed Tony's mind that Baldwin had set up the accident.

As the police car came to a standstill alongside his, the other driver's frustration and exuberance at being the centre of attention heightened. By this time Tony's own frustration bordered on red alert. Because of the language barrier, if his other disastrous encounters were anything to go by, things could get worse. He'd have trouble explaining his side of the story to the cops.

Two slightly built officers approached him, their guns on view, tucked into their belts and their sleeves pushed up past the elbows.

One of them had his notebook out and ready, and the older of the two men demanded to know—in French, of course—what had happened. If they did speak any English, Tony got the impression they had no intention of using it. He leaned against his hired car and watched, nonplussed, the exchange taking place between the coppers and the careless driver.

Out of the blue, a smartly dressed, well-coiffed woman in her early thirties said, voice raised, "*Non…*" The area fell silent, and everyone turned to face the woman, who was wearing a 'Don't mess with me' expression on her heavily made-up face.

"*Madame?*" asked the younger officer.

The woman stepped into the road and approached them. She turned to the careless driver and wagged her finger in his face. Every now and then, she looked or pointed in Tony's direction. After she'd finished her rant, the woman turned to Tony and explained in perfect English: "I told the officers that the old man came out of the turning without stopping. That he did not check to see if the road was clear. I saw the incident from the hairdresser's opposite. You were not at fault, *monsieur*. This man is an idiot, and I told 'im so. I do not like to see the English taken advantage of. My husband is English, and we see it a lot around here."

"I'm very grateful. Would you mind translating for me? I'd like to know if I'm going to be charged with an offence, or if I am free to continue my urgent journey."

"Of course. A moment please." Her face softened slightly to match her tone, and she explained Tony's position to the officers. The old man had the decency to look ashamed, the officers nodded a lot and then the woman addressed him once more. "Okay, they say you are free to go, but first you must show them your driver's licence and rental agreement for the car. They will be charging the old man for careless or reckless driving. I'm sorry, *monsieur*, for any inconvenience caused. You should be on your way soon."

"I'm most grateful, *madame*. You have restored my faith in the French people."

The woman blushed and went on her way. Half an hour later, Tony was free to go too. The first thing he did was contact Headquarters to see how far ahead Baldwin's car was. They told him the Lexus had been travelling at the speed limit and didn't appear to be in any kind of rush, which was good news for Tony; they also told him they had an inclination that Baldwin was heading for St

Etienne, the nearest big town. That would break Baldwin's journey on his way down to Monaco.

Tony glanced at his watch, four thirty PM. *Only another hour's worth of September daylight left.* Putting his foot down, he resumed the chase.

* * *

An uncomfortable silence filled the plush car. Lorne had her head leaning against the window, pretending to be asleep. She'd maintained that same position for the past few hours. Her nose remained sore, but at least it had stopped bleeding.

During the drive, Baldwin had continually run his hand up and down her slender thigh and even searched out her groin on several occasions, but somehow she'd managed to prevent herself from flinching. She'd tried to use the time well, thinking up several ways to get herself out of her dire situation. Unfortunately, most of the scenarios she'd come up with involved some form of weapon to aid her, which she clearly didn't have.

Her thoughts had been interspersed with prayers, too. She had prayed that Tony would track her down with reinforcements, and she also prayed her father would carry out his threat and call for backup if she forgot to ring him on time. After experiencing Baldwin's brutality first-hand, thoughts of Charlie popped up, causing her further pain and anguish. She had no trouble imagining the terror and fear her darling teenage daughter must have gone through the previous year and again marvelled at how well Charlie had shrugged off her ordeal since.

The car slowed down and took the next exit off the motorway. Lorne pretended to stir and yawned.

Baldwin leaned towards her, pressing his athletic body up against hers and whispered, "Nice sleep?"

Lorne's hand balled into a fist and she swallowed back more bile. She wanted to ask where they were heading, but the thought of receiving another punch to her already broken nose stopped her. Instead, she did as she was told and responded to his question. "Yes."

His hand once again reached between her thighs and rubbed back and forth, sending her body rigid with fear. Her eyes automatically closed, but she could have kicked herself when her actions gave

Baldwin the wrong impression.

"Enjoying that are you?" he asked, voice hushed.

She tried to lift her leg, but his thumb dug into her thigh, forcing it to drop back down. His hand intensified its intrusion, and she was powerless to stop it.

"That's right, Lorne, resist the urge to strike out. I'll take what I want with or without your permission."

Her nails dug into the palms of both her hands, and a shiver she could no longer hold back swept through her body. *Oh God, please somebody rescue me soon.*

Baldwin removed his hand as the car came to a standstill outside another plush hotel at their destination, the Inter-Hotel Actuel. Lorne noticed an airport sign further up the road and wondered if that had any connection with Baldwin's choice of that particular hotel in St Etienne. Within seconds of them stopping, Lorne was yanked across the back seat and out onto the bustling pavement. They stepped into the boutique hotel, Baldwin's arm wrapped around her shoulder. "Any crap, and you'll end up like Renée. Smile and at least look as if you're enjoying yourself." He dug his fingers into her shoulder and guided her through the marbled floor reception area and over to the front desk.

"*Bonjour, monsieur et madame. Avez-vous une réservation?*"

"No. My wife and I would like a room for one night only."

"Ah, you are English. Of course, a suite or a double room?"

Baldwin turned and smiled. "I think a suite, don't you, darling?"

A forced smile lit up her face, and Lorne nodded eagerly at her fake husband.

Baldwin turned back to the receptionist. "My wife is kind of shy—it's our honeymoon, you see."

Lorne's stomach dropped when the pretty brunette tapped the side of her nose and winked at Lorne. "I understand completely, I am a newlywed myself too. I will give you this room. It is empty either side, so you will not be disturbed." The receptionist chuckled, turned her back, and plucked a key attached to a gold key ring from the board behind and placed it on the counter in front of them.

Dumb bitch. Can't you see there is something wrong with my nose? Lorne peered over his shoulder to see what Baldwin was writing on the reservation form and felt sick. *Mr. and Mrs. Smith.*

With the false smile still stretched across her face, Lorne followed the bellboy into the lift, Baldwin one step behind her, watching her every move. When the young man opened the door to the suite and stepped back allowing them to enter, Lorne couldn't help being amazed at the size of it. Its grandeur was something she'd never experienced before, anywhere.

Baldwin tipped and dismissed the bellboy, and Lorne's fear rose again. The thought of being alone with Baldwin made her skin crawl. She wiped away a bead of sweat running down her cheek. Her abductor laughed, enjoying her obvious signs of discomfort.

"Why don't we make ourselves comfortable? Would you like a drink?"

Lorne shuddered. She didn't know what side of him she liked less. At least when he was being nasty and punching her, she knew where she stood. The more pleasant, caring side he was portraying left her feeling as though she had a block of ice taped to her back. She shook her head, determined to leave her mind clear, alert and ready to pounce on any chance of escape that may arise.

Baldwin's gaze narrowed, and he studied her before opening up the mini-bar. He took a few miniature bottles of vodka and tipped them into two glasses. He brought them over to her and handed her one. *"Drink it."*

His tone warned of what would happen should she refuse the drink. Her hand shook as she took the glass, despite her best efforts not to show how scared she was, being in the same room with him, alone. Baldwin's eyes sparkled with amusement. He downed his drink in one gulp and glared at her, expecting her to do the same. She knocked her drink back, suppressing the burning sensation as it hit the back of her throat.

Baldwin laughed. "Granted, not the best vodka I've tasted, but it'll do." The smile disappeared from his handsome face, and fear shot through Lorne again when he said, "Now, get undressed."

Chapter Thirty-Seven

As he drove towards St Etienne, Tony debated whether or not he should ring Sam Collins. He had already told Headquarters he needed reinforcements, and they'd agreed to send two more agents to help. *Wow, two more!* Against the number of men Baldwin had, they'd be lucky if everyone got out of the operation intact.

As he approached a green sign telling him his destination was only nine kilometres ahead, Tony decided Lorne's father had a right to know she was missing. He reached into her handbag that was lying in the passenger footwell, grabbed her phone and searched through the numbers. He found the listing for "Dad" and placed the call.

"Lorne! Everything all right?"

Tony cleared his throat. "Er… Mr. Collins…"

"Who is this? Why are you using my daughter's phone? Warner, is that you?"

"It is, Sam…"

"Well? For Christ's sake, man. Tell me what's happened?" Fear filled Sam's voice.

Tony briefly contemplated how he should proceed. He was aware how close Lorne was to her father. "First of all, I want to assure you that everything is in hand. I've called for backup—"

"Warner, just tell me! I want to know everything."

So he told the man everything. Tony didn't feel the need to disguise how dire the situation was. Sam Collins was an ex-copper, after all.

He heard the man expel the breath he'd been holding in, then grunt a little, as if he'd sunk into a chair. "Sam? You all right?" he queried, concerned for the older man's health.

"I'm catching the first flight out. I know you want to stay on their tail, so don't bother telling me you'll meet me. You say you think they're heading for Monaco?"

Tony thumped the steering wheel. *This is the last thing I want.* If Sam came out, Tony would feel duty-bound to look after him, and that would mean he wouldn't be able to put as much effort into finding or rescuing Lorne. He tried his best to dissuade him, but Sam had other ideas, and it was obvious to Tony whom Lorne had inherited her stubborn streak from.

"Okay, Sam, you win. I reckon they'll reach the coast in a few days, probably on Thursday. I could arrange for a car to meet you at the airport in Nice. It's not far from there. I'll get the driver to bring you to the hotel where I'll be staying. How does that sound?"

"I appreciate it, Tony. You understand my need to be there, don't you?"

"Completely. Make the arrangements and then get back to me. And, Sam?"

"Yes?"

"Try not to worry about Lorne. You know what a tough girl she is. I'm sure he won't hurt her."

There was a pause before Sam spoke again. "We'll see, Tony. I hope you're right, though. Speak soon."

They both hung up, and as Tony concentrated on driving through his ever-darkening surroundings, he wondered about the accuracy of his words. Would Lorne be all right? Did she have enough balls and willpower to overcome anything the Unicorn was about to throw at her?

* * *

Lorne stood stark naked before Baldwin. Her hands tried to shield her pubic area from his searching, amused eyes.

"Funny, that… Your daughter didn't hide her modesty when she was standing naked in front of me." He laughed, carefully watching her reaction. "Mind you she didn't really get the chance to, what with my men holding her down whi—"

"You disgusting pig!" she shrieked and ran at him. She pounded her fists on his puffed-out chest.

Baldwin held firm and allowed her a few thumps before he grabbed both her wrists and squashed them in one of his giant hands. Lorne stopped struggling, finding the pain unbearable, so bad she thought one of her bones would snap any second. His other hand stroked its way up and down her nakedness, pausing now and then as he watched her expressions alternate between fear, pain, and hatred.

"Shall I show you how *disgusting* I can be, Lorne?" he asked, his words full of undisguised meaning.

153

She gulped noisily and pleaded with her eyes. But as he reached into the pocket of his black suit trousers and pulled out a small tin the size of a Golden Virginia Tobacco tin her grandfather used to carry, she knew no matter what sort of fight she put up against Baldwin, there would only ever be one outcome. He had a strength she had never come across before. *You idiot, of course he has. He was SAS, wasn't he?*

"Please, no drugs... I won't cause you any more trouble... Please."

He smirked and flicked off the lid to the tin with his thumb, revealing a syringe and a small vial of clear liquid. Her heart sank, and her stomach knotted.

She realised it wouldn't be possible for him to inject her given their positions, but Baldwin seemed to have the same idea. Before she knew what was happening he'd thrown her face down on the bed. Quickly she scampered up to the headboard and covered herself with one of the pillows. Baldwin's face registered annoyance as he filled the syringe, whilst keeping half an eye on Lorne.

"No. Please... I'm begging you!' Lorne decided to play the role of a damsel in distress, while her mind actively searched for a way out of her difficult situation.

"As they say in all the best *Carry On* films, Lorne, you'll only feel a little prick." His satanic laughter filled the room. As he walked towards the bed, she cowered as if scared of him, but inside, her determination was growing with every passing second. Closer and closer he came, a knowing smirk twisting his mouth.

Wait, not yet. Be patient. With one hand clutching at the pillow shielding her body, she reached behind her and felt for the lamp. Baldwin's eyes were fixed on hers; the brass base of the lamp felt cold to her touch.

He climbed onto the bed and kept coming towards her. Lorne dropped the pillow to hold his attention. His lecherous eyes dropped to Lorne's breasts. She took the opportunity and grabbed the lamp. *Thump!* Baldwin slumped onto her legs as the heavy base connected with his skull.

Shit, that wasn't supposed to happen. Thankfully, Baldwin was out cold. How long that would last was anybody's guess. Lorne pushed at the heavy man at the same time she tried to free her legs from under him. Panting from her exertions, she finally broke free, ran over to her clothes, and quickly threw them on, keeping an eye on Baldwin lying face down on the bed, blood seeping from the side of his head.

Finding it hard to believe she'd succeeded in escaping his clutches, Lorne eased open the door, exhaling with relief when she saw the corridor was empty. She'd expected at least one of Baldwin's men to be standing on guard outside. After pulling the door closed behind her, she walked swiftly down the hallway and jumped into the lift. *Hope his goons aren't hanging around downstairs.*

The doors slid back to reveal an almost empty reception area. Rather than ask for help from the receptionist, Lorne ran out of the hotel and into the chilly evening. The street was aglow from the nearby streetlights.

Panic gnawed her insides. She ducked down a narrow side road and followed an old man in a beret accompanied by an old lady pulling a shopping trolley behind her, up a slight hill.

"*Excusez-moi,*" Lorne mumbled, as she squeezed past the pair of them. The man touched his hat and said something in French that she didn't understand. She smiled and continued down the narrow street, past the backyards, some of which had barking dogs running around warding off would-be intruders, until she came to the opening that lead to a busy main road.

Looking first one way then the other, she decided going to the right would be her best option. There was much more traffic travelling in that direction, which was always a good indication, something her father had taught her years ago when she'd first passed her driving test in case she ever got lost.

Lorne cautiously walked down the crowded pavement, dipping into the odd shop doorway pretending to admire their wares, before glancing back in the direction she'd come from keeping an eye open for Baldwin or his men. With the coast clear, she set off again in search of a public telephone.

Ten minutes later, she located a telephone outside a local Tabac. The next dilemma she needed to overcome was how she would pay for the call. Her bag and purse were back in the car with Tony. Frantically she hunted through every pocket, but to no avail.

"*Madame?*"

A voice startled her. Slowly she turned to face a middle-aged man giving her a puzzled look.

Wracking her brain, she attempted to recall the few phrases of

French she knew, "*Parlez-vous Anglaise?*"

"Fortunately for you, yes." He smiled and put her at ease. "Do you need money for the telephone?"

"Would you mind?"

He dug in the pocket of his suit trousers and came out with a handful of centimes. "Take what you want, *madame*."

Hesitantly, Lorne messed around with the coins in his palm, but she had no idea which one she needed to make a call to England. She intended ringing her father, back in London. Tony's number was a speed dial on her mobile, so she didn't have a clue what it was. "If it's not too much trouble, I need to ring England,"

Shrugging, he handed her a euro coin.

She took it and dialled. She tapped her foot as the phone rang several times before her father picked up. "Oh, Dad. Thank God you're home."

"Lorne? Where are you? How…"

"Dad, I haven't got time to answer your questions. I need help."

"I know. Tony's been in touch. I'm flying out tomorr—"

"No, Dad. Please, don't come out here. I'm fine—I've escaped—but I need to get in touch with Tony quickly. I was wondering if you could ring MI5 HQ for me?"

"No need for that, love, I have his number right here. Can you hold the line while I ring him on my mobile?"

"Be quick, Dad. I haven't much money. I'm in St. Etienne."

Lorne turned to face the man again, exchanged smiles with him, and then cast a worried eye up the road. *Surely Baldwin must have woken up by now and alerted his goons!*

"Lorne?"

"I'm here, Dad."

"Tony's in the town now. Is there a landmark nearby where you can wait for him?"

She glanced over her shoulder and saw the large building with a yellow sign off to the right. "That's brilliant, Dad. Tell him to wait outside the post office for me. If I'm not there when he arrives, tell him to be patient. I'll probably be hiding in a bush or something just in case Baldwin or his men come looking for me." She heard him relay her message to Tony.

"Lorne, the minute Tony picks you up, I want you back on a plane heading home ASAP, do you hear me?"

"I hear you, Dad, but you know that ain't going to happen."

"Right, then we'll both be bloody-minded. I'm flying out tomorrow, and I'll catch up with you in Monaco. Until then stay safe, darling."

Before she had the chance to argue, he'd hung up.

Lorne thanked her knight in shining armour for coming to her rescue and shook his hand.

The man gave her a concerned look. "I insist that I come with you."

So there are people willing to help a damsel in distress, after all. She smiled, patted the man on the arm, and shook her head. "Thank you for your kindness. I'm a policewoman. I cannot put a civilian in danger." Hoping the lie would deter the stranger from getting involved, she turned and ran down the road.

A few minutes later, she arrived at the post office but felt too exposed standing outside the agreed rendezvous point and quickly ducked behind a parked delivery van. Her neck soon ached from constantly searching all around her, but her panic turned to joy when Tony pulled up outside the large stone building.

After collapsing into the passenger seat beside the agent, she let out a large breath. "Boy, am I glad to see you."

"Not half as glad as I am to see you," he said. "Jesus, Lorne. What did that fucker do to you? Let's get you to a doctor." She shook her head adamantly. He gathered her in his arms and whispered, "He didn't r—rape you, did he?"

Lorne thought about Charlie's experience at the hands of Baldwin and released a relieved breath. "No. Thank God."

Chapter Thirty-Eight

After booking into a less luxurious hotel than the one Baldwin had taken her to, Lorne and Tony entered their room and stood by the door wordlessly staring at each other.

The moment lasted for what seemed like hours. Tony was the first to react. He gently grabbed her by the wrist and slowly pulled her towards him.

Lorne felt self-conscious about the way she looked, with her torn clothes and bloody face, and although Tony eyed her with sympathy, she knew he was too much of a gent to tell her how awful she looked. He lowered his head, their lips barely touching before his tongue began its searching, probing journey.

A satisfying moan caught in her throat that seemed to amuse Tony.

She pulled away from him. "Something funny, agent boy?"

Instead of getting annoyed like he usually did when she called him the detested name, he took a step back and placed one hand behind her knees and swept her off her feet. Seconds later, he placed her gently on the bed and froze.

Her puzzlement disappeared when she understood the meaning of his hesitation. Her hand stroked the side of his face. She smiled when he trapped it with his own, turned it over, and started kissing and licking her palm. An involuntary shiver rippled through her body. Desperate to feel him on top of her, Lorne grabbed him by the lapels and slowly pulled him down.

"You're beautiful." His lips trailed down her throat, causing her to arch her hips and let out a sigh. His impatient hands tugged at her jacket and shook as he undid the tiny pearl-shaped buttons on her blouse.

"Oh, Tony," she whispered, as his mouth sought out the mound of her breast and slipped around her nipple. Her desire level went through the ceiling. Urgently she tore off his jacket before ripping open his shirt, not giving a second thought to the fact that they were travelling light and his shirts were in short supply. She ran her hands down his taut chest, past his flat stomach, and found the zip of his trousers. She eased down the zipper, and with a shaking hand, she searched out the opening. Tony paused, anticipating her next move.

Diving past the folds of his boxers, Lorne stroked a teasing finger up and down his erection, making him suck in a deep breath. Finding the whole seduction scenario too much to take, Tony ripped off the rest of her clothes and his, throwing them in a pile on the floral patterned carpet.

"I've wanted you for so long," he whispered in her ear before his lips trailed a seductive line down her trembling body, past her breasts, down over her stomach. He kissed her hip bones, begging not to be forgotten, before finally ending up at her very core.

With his tongue probing and his teeth nibbling the sensitive area, Lorne's hands gripped and twisted the cover of the bed on either side of her. Her heart thumped loudly. Finally, she uttered the words she sensed Tony was longing to hear. "Please, take me, Tony. Please."

He entered her with the ease of a well-oiled piece of machinery, lubricated and ready to perform. Tony towered above her, and the changing expressions covering his face fascinated her.

The way his eyes clenched shut amused Lorne slightly. "Tony, look at me," she ordered, feeling masterful and in charge of her fate.

His eyelids opened, and his eyes glistened with desire.

She smiled shyly, feeling suddenly insecure. Blushing, she turned to look at the wall to her right.

Tony paused. "What's wrong?" A single tear slipped down her face.

The next thing she knew, he had slipped out of her and was tenderly gathering her in his arms. "Lorne? What's up?"

She didn't respond.

His finger tipped under her chin and pulled her head round to face him. "Don't shut me out, hon."

"I'm so sorry, Tony. I want this so much, but…"

Propping himself up on his elbow, he ran his forefinger down her cheek with the gentlest of touches, and his thumb wiped away the tear that had settled there. "Then what's the problem?"

Lorne hesitated. Looking into his eyes, she felt a pang of guilt as she saw the concern evident in their depths. "He was going to rape me."

"What?!" Tony shouted. He sat up and dragged his fingers down his face, then returned to his position beside her, dragging Lorne into his arms again and placing her head on his chest. "But he didn't?" he asked more softly.

For the first time that day, she felt safe, safe and relieved that she hadn't come to any serious harm, like Charlie had when Baldwin abducted her. She started to play with the soft hairs on his chest and shook her head. "No, thank goodness. He had a needle full of clear liquid—probably heroin—he was about to inject me with, but I managed to hit him with a lamp. We were staying in a posh suite, luckily. The lamp was made of brass, so the impact turned out to be substantial."

"Ouch!"

"I was so scared. I can't believe I even thought of fighting him."

"It was probably a combination of things that motivated you. Seeing that he was about to drug and rape you, and then there was the contributing factor of the hatred you felt for him because of the way he treated your daughter. A mother's love and instincts to protect or avenge more than likely came into play."

"It kind of brought it all home to me what Charlie had to contend with last year. I'm so proud of the way she's handled everything."

"She's obviously riddled with your brave genes." Tony laughed as his hand stroked her arm sending flames of desire running through her.

"What happens now?"

"Well, the minute I realised he had taken you, I rang London. They're sending out a few agents to help. I'll keep quiet about you escaping until tomorrow. Otherwise, they might deploy the agents elsewhere. I'd like to bring Baldwin down, once and for all, and the more reinforcements we have out here to do that, the better. Now, how about we get some sleep?"

She looked up at him, desire written in her face. "How about we don't?"

He grinned and didn't need asking twice.

Chapter Thirty-Nine

The following morning, a loud thumping on their hotel room door woke Lorne and her new lover.

"Jesus! It's nearly ten." Tony gave Lorne a quick kiss on the lips before jumping out of bed to put on his trousers.

She stretched under the covers and smiled at him. "I take it a repeat of last night's action is out of the question, then?"

The glint in her eye and her teasing smile must have amused Tony, as he leapt on to the bed again. "You little minx. I can see you getting me into severe trouble. As much as I'd love to make love to you again, I have a feeling that's the reinforcements at the door. Now, get your amazingly firm arse out of this bed and into the bathroom, and don't forget to take your clothes with you." He winked. "And we'll sort out the encore later. That's a promise." He tore back the bedclothes and ran his love-filled eyes over her naked body, somehow resisting the temptation to jump on her again by shoving her out of the bed.

Lorne wiggled her way towards the bathroom, picking up her clothes en route. Before entering the bathroom, she paused and looked back over her shoulder to see if he was watching her. She needn't have worried. He appeared transfixed by the movement of her body, and the bulge in his trousers made it obvious he was enjoying the show.

* * *

Another thunderous knock on the door brought Tony's focus back to getting dressed. He threw on his blue shirt, leaving it hanging out on purpose, hoping to disguise his erection; he squeezed his eyes shut as the shower started, anticipating he was about to receive the ribbing of his life from his colleagues.

When he threw open the door, two men, both in their mid-twenties, were standing either side of it, arms folded, their heads resting against the doorframe, knowing smiles on their smug faces.

"Busy were you, Warner?"

"Fuck off, Taylor." He stood back, and both men entered the room, their eyes glued to the messed-up bed. *Shit! This is all I need. This will keep these guys in ammunition for bloody months.* "We were forced to share a bed—lack of funds from HQ—and it was the only room available when we booked in late last night."

"Who're you trying to fucking kid? So you got her back then, when?" Distrust coloured Weir's face.

"Yeah, and she was damn lucky to escape from the bastard. I— well, her father, actually—got a call from her about twelve last night."

"Nice and convenient!"

"Your point is, Weir?"

The agent shrugged and sat down on the end of the bed. "Just saying… Haven't got us out here under false pretences, I hope, Warner?"

They all glanced at the bathroom door when they heard the shower stop. Taylor muttered, "Can't wait to see what all the fuss is about."

"All right, you two fucking behave yourselves when she comes out, do you hear me?"

"Or?" Weir asked, stretching his legs out.

"Cut the crap. We need to get this guy, and there's no way on this earth I could manage that alone. You're here now, so stop the whinging, okay? Is HQ still tracking his vehicle?"

"As far as I know. I've got to tell them we've located you and the girl anyway. I'll make the call." Taylor went back out into the hallway and left Warner and Weir eyeing each other cautiously.

"Come on, then. Let's have it, Weir?" Tony propped himself up against the dressing table and crossed his arms in front of him.

"I think we've been down this road before, mate, haven't we?"

"This is different. Lorne and I know where we stand. She knows the job—"

The bathroom door opened, and Lorne breezed into the room, her shoulders back and ready for a fight.

"Don't stop now, Tony. The conversation was just getting interesting." She stopped in front of the man lounging on the bed, her arm outstretched, ready to shake his hand.

Weir accepted her hand with a shocked look and a half-smile.

Still holding her hand, Weir rose from the bed. "Pleased to meet you, Lorne. You had us worried there for a while. Glad to see you back safe. You were lucky to have escaped from Baldwin. Hope he came off worse than you in the fight?"

"He did, I assure you. You were *worried*? Well, that's good to know." She removed her hand from his and forced a smile. "You were saying, Tony?"

Tony wore his strongest poker face, and his eyes remained firmly on hers. But Lorne simply smiled at him and pushed him aside to retrieve the dryer out of the dressing table drawer. Both men watched her trundle back into the bathroom, acting as though she didn't have a care in the world.

Weir shook his head and mumbled, "I rest my case."

Before Tony could fight his corner again, a sullen-faced Taylor came back into the room.

"What's up?" Tony asked, his concern matching that of his colleague.

"It's Baldwin... He's gone already."

"What? When?" Tony and Weir asked at the same time.

Taylor's eyes narrowed and zeroed in on Tony. "Probably while you were screwing her ladyship in—"

Weir stepped between Taylor and Tony.

"Fuck off, Taylor. Just give us the facts, without the wisecracks," Tony demanded.

The three men turned to face Lorne when she opened the bathroom door and wandered back into the relatively small room, her hair dried. She'd disguised her black eyes with heavy makeup. "What?" she asked puzzled.

Tony nodded for Taylor to continue, "Baldwin left his hotel in the early hours of this morning," he turned to Tony and stated his voice full of accusation. "Apparently, HQ has been trying to contact you every hour on the hour since."

Lorne blushed, and Tony dashed to his phone, which was sitting on the small bedside table. He let out a heavy breath and threw the phone on the bed. "Bloody battery is dead. Don't look at me like that, you two. I found Lorne well after midnight—badly beaten as you can see. And by the time she went over what had happened..."

"Stop! Tony, you shouldn't have to make excuses for me. If you guys don't believe what went on here last night, then that's your problem, not ours." She jutted out her breasts stubbornly, and then folded her arms when she realised the three men were focused on her slightly exposed cleavage.

Weir retorted under his breath, "Guess it's our fault Baldwin's got away again, is it? Mind you, you should be used to that—"

"All right, Weir, that was uncalled for. Arguing amongst ourselves isn't getting us anywhere. Taylor, have HQ got a location on Baldwin?" Tony asked.

"He was last spotted going past the junction for Orange on the A7, approximately two hundred twenty kilometres from here. Showing no signs of stopping, either."

Taylor had a map in his hand, and Tony took it from him, studied it for a few moments. "That's strange. He usually takes a break every few hundred kilometres. Wonder what that's all about?"

Lorne suggested, "Consider this. Every time he's stopped, something has happened." She hesitated as the men contemplated her idea, looking perplexed. It wasn't until Tony gave her a quick nod, urging her to carry on, that she continued, "When we stopped at Le Mans, the *lieutenant*'s body was found. Then he abducted me. Makes you wonder if he's playing games with us, or warning us?"

"You have a point, Lorne. Maybe he's meeting up with someone further on and he's rushing to get there. Have you guys got a rental car?"

"Yep," Weir answered. "We better get on the move before he connects with anyone else. You guys get things sorted here and check out. We'll try to locate some breakfast for all of us, meet up again outside in what, ten minutes?"

After the two agents left the room, Tony walked over to Lorne and gathered her in his arms. She released a comforting sigh as her head came to rest on his chest.

"Hey, ignore their leg pulling. They're harmless enough. You all ready to go?"

Lorne smiled up at him. "It'll take me a few minutes to pack my bag and Tony…"

Head tilted, his eyes asked the question.

"Don't worry about the guys. I might have taken a year off work, but coming up with suitable put-downs is built-in, something that'll never abandon me. Don't forget the 'pigs' I had to deal with in the MET, no pun intended. What I'm trying to say is, don't feel as though you need to jump to my defence all the time."

Their lips met, lingering for a few moments before Tony pulled away. Smiling, he twisted her around and patted her gently on the backside. "As much as I'd love to continue this, I think capturing

Baldwin should be at the top of our list of priorities." He picked up his bag, placed it on the bed and within seconds had zipped it up and announced, "I'll go settle the bill. Two minutes, okay?"

Lorne mock-saluted him and intentionally wiggled her backside, then watched him walk out of the hotel room. She felt as though she was walking on air when she marched into the bathroom to pack her travel bag.

Eyeing her reflection in the small mirror above the sink, she shook her head and warned, "You'll be foolish to get involved, girl. Ha... Since when did I listen to you?"

Chapter Forty

The two-car convoy sped through the French countryside, staying just under the speed limit. The last thing they needed was to get picked up for speeding. Between them, they decided Tony would lead in his car, while Taylor and Weir would be the ones to remain in contact with Headquarters. Any news gathered would be passed via Tony's fully recharged mobile.

Lorne had been given the job of answering Tony's phone. "Hello?" Tony glanced sideways as she listened and nodded her head to what the caller had to say. "Okay, I'll let Tony know."

"Was it Taylor?"

"Yep, Baldwin is still on the A7. He's just passed Avignon. He thinks we've made up some ground on him, according to London he's now approximately one hundred fifty kilometres ahead of us."

"That's a good sign, I suppose."

"He's still a good way ahead of us, though."

"What are you thinking? I've been keeping an eye on you for the past half-hour or so, and you've been so deep in thought you haven't noticed."

Their gazes met briefly before Tony turned his attention back to the road.

Lorne smiled. "There's no flies on you, is there? I was mulling over a few possibilities, that's all. A few *What if?*s, like 'What if he's leading us into one of his notorious traps?' The last time he did that, I lost my partner." A picture of Pete's chubby face and cheeky smile forced its way into her mind, and her eyes misted over. She remained silent for a moment, then took a tissue from a pack lying on the seat, and blew her nose carefully. The image of Pete brought with it intense sadness and loss to her heart. "I still miss him." She sniffled.

Tony gently squeezed her hand and reassured her. "Lorne, you have three MI6 agents watching your back, this time round."

She released a long sigh. "There is that, I suppose. Last time he abducted me, there was only the one." He withdrew his hand sharply, expression offended. "Sorry, it was meant as a joke. A poor one, admittedly."

His frown vanished, replaced by a small smile. "What other 'what if's did you think of?"

"Thinking back, I'm wondering if the *lieutenant* was the only one involved with Baldwin's plans…"

"Go on."

"What if you were right about the *capitaine* all along? What if they used Renée as a scapegoat, a convenience who had outlived her usefulness?"

"I'm glad you finally agree with me about the smarmy Frenchman, but there's little we can do about that now."

"Oh, I don't know. Has MI6 delved into his past?"

"I think they carried out a small background search on the guy, nothing too deep. When we stop again, I'll ring and ask them to dig deeper into his record."

"Umm…With respect, Tony, that might be too late. What about me placing the call for you?"

"Dial the number. It's on speed dial seven, then I'll talk to HQ on the hands-free."

Without hesitating, Lorne dialled the number, and Tony issued the order to London, who told him they would get back to him within a few hours.

With all the *What if?*s dealt with, and the day turning into night, Lorne decided to try to catch up on some of the sleep she'd missed out on the night before. Sleep came easily to her, despite the drone of the engine as Tony raced along the A7 in pursuit of Baldwin. But within half an hour, she was fully awake, as Baldwin's vile features and his intentions back at the hotel infiltrated her dream.

"Nice sleep?"

"Hardly. I just can't seem to get away from the image of that bastard…"

"Try not to dwell on it, Lorne. I know it's easier said than done, but this time, we'll nab him, for sure. The team we have now has more than thirty years' experience of covert operations under their belts."

His words reassured her, but before she could respond, Tony's mobile rang, and Lorne answered it.

"Okay, I'll let Tony know." She dropped the phone back into her lap. "Taylor says Baldwin has turned onto the A8 at Aix-en-

Provence, still on course for Monaco."

She pulled the map from the passenger door pocket and pointed out the location. With forefinger and thumb touching, she stretched them to measure the distance. "I estimate we're about one-eighty or one-ninety kilometres away."

Tony squinted thoughtfully and quickly made some calculations. "Approximately two hours, then, give or take."

"Then what?"

"That, dear Lorne, is the sixty-four thousand dollar question."

The car remained silent until they reached their destination.

The bright lights of Monaco beckoned and guided them like a lighthouse, aiding a distressed ship into port. Tony pulled the car into a car park situated in front of the marina, which lived up to its name of being a billionaire's playground, if the display of expensive yachts was anything to go by.

No sooner had they stopped than did both rear doors open, and Taylor and Weir jumped in the back. "Any idea what his boat is called?" Taylor asked, resting his head back and blowing out a tired sigh.

Lorne responded, echoing the agent's tiredness, *"Lady Luck."*

Taylor telephoned Headquarters straight away. "Miles, Yeah, it's me. We're sitting in the marina car park. Any idea what's happened with Baldwin?" He paused for a few moments, then said, "I see," and hung up. "Okay, well, apparently they already knew the name of his boat from the satellite."

He paused, picked up the binoculars he'd removed from the seat when he first entered the car, and angled them out to sea. "Sweet as a nut! There she be."

The others in the car followed Taylor's pointing finger, past the harbour walls out to the yacht.

"Jesus Christ, that baby is huge!' Weir gave a whistle of admiration.

Her face etched with worry, Lorne turned to Tony. "He's right… It's huge."

"What's your point, Lorne?" he asked, frowning.

"My point is, even from this distance, I can tell that boat is far bigger than the one he managed to escape on last year. You know… Abromovski's boat, the one with the garage on-board that concealed the submarine he used to evade us." Her tone was that of a defeated Army officer surrounded by his dead squad of men.

Tony contemplated her proclamation for a moment. "Okay, I get where you're coming from, but there are four of us... three who are highly-trained in covert operations."

"Oh, well, that's all right then. Problem solved." Lorne laughed.

"Sarcasm isn't going to help," Tony bit back.

"Now, now, we don't want—or need—a lover's tiff, you guys," Weir joked.

"Fuck off, Weir. I'm being serious here," Tony snapped.

"That's the problem, Tony. So am I. Think about it, will you? That boat is going to be crawling with staff. Okay, there might be four of us, but I reckon there'll be... On a yacht that size? At least twenty, possibly even thirty, staff."

"I hate to admit it—"

Lorne twisted in her seat to glare at Taylor.

"I mean, she's probably right about that," Taylor corrected himself. "No, she's not *probably* right. She *is* right."

"Okay, this is what I suggest we do: We'll find a nearby hotel, get a few hours' rest." Tony touched the button on the side of his watch, and its face lit up. "It's just coming up to ten now. We could reconvene in, say, four hours? You're not going to tell me the staff will be in full force at two in the morning. That's if they're there at all yet—don't forget, he's only just arrived."

Everyone agreed, and Taylor and Weir left the car. Tony took Lorne's hand in his. Their gazes met, and he whispered, "Hey, don't ever forget I'm on your side in this."

With eyelids lowered, she bowed her head, chin almost touching her collarbone. She felt her cheeks burn and appreciated the darkness of the car.

Tony nudged her chin upwards, expression puzzled. When he brushed her lips with his, she pulled away and shifted uncomfortably in her seat. She had to pull away; she couldn't let herself depend on him. "Sorry, Tony. I'm just tired. Didn't you mention something about getting a hotel room or rooms?"

His hurt feelings evident, Tony started the car and headed back into town.

Chapter Forty-One

Again, when Lorne and Tony reached the hotel—despite his best efforts—they were forced to share another hotel room and yet another double bed. Neither of them had spoken since their strange moment in the car. They went to the bathroom, one after the other, then slid into bed, still quiet.

Lorne teetered on the edge of her side, making a conscious effort not to relax and touch Tony's body with any part of her own. She felt foolish for the way she had reacted to his kiss. She had to put a halt to things, before either of them became dependent on the other. Actually, thinking about her situation, it was more a case of breaking things off before *she* became dependent on *him.*

A thump on the door woke them, and still feeling nervous from her recent ordeal, Lorne sat up in bed with the bedclothes pulled tightly under her chin, like she had done as a little girl when she thought the bogeyman would get her, in her often vivid nightmares.

When Tony turned on the light, she could tell by his face he thought she was losing her mind. Before he opened the door, he asked tersely, "You all right?"

Embarrassed, she threw back the covers and ran into the bathroom, snatching up her bag en route.

She emerged fully clothed around ten minutes later, to find Taylor and Weir sitting on the bed and Tony standing in front of them, with a pad and pen in his hand.

Tony indicated for Lorne to stand alongside him and handed her the notebook. When she'd finished reading, she looked at Tony and shrugged. "Looks all in order, except one thing."

He took back the pad, scanned what was written, and looked at Lorne again, brow furrowed. "One thing?"

"That's right…" she said.

"Hello, people. Time is of the essence here. Any chance we can rush things along a little?" Weir impatiently tapped his watch.

Annoyed that Tony hadn't spotted his mistake, Lorne folded her arms. "My role in this mission?"

The two other agents sniggered.

She glared at them. "Gentlemen? Do you have a problem?"

Weir smirked. "Hey, you guys can keep us out of your little argument. Taylor and I will see if we can pick up some food in this God-forsaken metropolis for the rich and shallow people, while you two 'talk things over'. Just don't take long discussing things. We need to strike before it's too late."

"Really, Weir, there's nothing to discuss. I have no intention of sitting around here, twiddling God knows what, while you three have all the fun." Lorne forced a smile, but Tony's face looked stormy. She cocked her head to the side and defiantly glared back at him.

Tony walked over to the door, opened it, and dismissed the two men. "We'll see you guys in a few minutes." He slammed the door shut after them.

"Was that called for? Slamming the door like that, at this ungodly hour of the morning?" Lorne backed up to the bed and collapsed on it. She had an inkling Tony was about to tear into her and rip her to tiny pieces.

"Sod what people think or are trying to do around here. Let's get one thing straight, Lorne: *You* are not stepping foot out of this hotel room. Have I made myself perfectly clear?"

She jumped to her feet, and they met halfway, toe to toe, her nose to his chest. She glared up at him. "About as clear as mud, *agent boy*!"

"Don't go there, Lorne."

Despite the warning resonating in his voice, Lorne challenged him further. "What good will I be sitting here?"

"If you stay here, then I know you're safe."

She opened her mouth to object, but Tony raised his hand to silence her. Before she knew what was happening, his long muscular arms swallowed her and pressed her against his chest. His scent filled her nostrils. A sense of calm and comfort burst through her, making her stubbornness recede.

Gazing up at him, she smiled and shrugged. "Okay, buster. I guess this is round one to you."

His lips pressed firmly against hers, and his tongue teased her lips apart. It was the deepest kiss she'd ever experienced, one that left her reeling with poorly timed cravings. From his reaction, she knew he felt the same way.

"Shit! I hate having to stop this here, but I need to get changed. The guys will be back soon."

Reluctantly, she left his arms and watched as he stripped off his clothes. She found it hard to restrain the growing sense of desire caressing her groin. When Tony had finished dressing in his black trousers and a black polo-neck jumper, he gathered her in his arms again and kissed her long and hard.

Lorne couldn't help wondering if he'd kissed her that way because he feared he wouldn't return. She brushed the feeling aside as quickly as it had appeared.

They had just broken apart when the hotel door opened and in stepped Taylor and Weir, dressed in the same outfits as Tony. Weir handed Tony a baguette filled with ham and cheese. Tony took the proffered snack and shared a quick smile with Lorne.

Frowning, Weir asked, "Something wrong?"

"Not really. I appreciate the thought, Weir. Thanks."

"Hurry up and eat it. We leave in ten. Sorry, Lorne. I didn't think to get you one, thought you could grab some breakfast later."

She waved her hand and grabbed the baguette from Tony. "No problem. I'll help Tony eat his."

Again, she shared an amused look with Tony, and Weir blew out a frustrated sigh.

"Whatever," Tony responded, noisily chomping on his extra-large piece of French stick as if he hadn't eaten in days. He was fatter than the other two men, and Lorne could see why, after watching him swallow his food without seeming to chew it.

Sadness drifted over her as memories of her dead partner visited again. Pete's nickname had been 'Chunky', not only due to his larger-than-average belly. He'd loved chunky Kit Kats.

Lorne found it strange that she still thought about him and wondered how long the memories would persist. He'd been a significant part of her life for nine years or so, before Baldwin had killed him in cold blood. Perhaps it was natural for her to often think of him, just a little.

Between mouthfuls of food, the men discussed final preparations then marched out of the room, with Lorne in hot pursuit.

Tony stopped and turned when he heard her steps behind him. "What the… Just a minute, young lady. I thought we'd gone over this?"

"I'm not coming with you—you made it quite clear my skills were not needed in this manoeuvre—but you can't stop me from coming down to the marina to see you off." She stubbornly jutted out her chin; he would be wasting precious time if he argued with her.

"Okay, you win again," he mumbled.

When Lorne stepped into the hallway, he shut the door then handed her the key.

Upon reaching the marina, the number of people dotted around so early in the morning surprised Lorne. None of them appeared to be drunk like people would have been in a busy town in England. No, the French were definitely more refined as far as alcohol was concerned.

Taylor and Weir took off in the direction of the first jetty, where they had arranged for a rowboat to be waiting for them.

"Take care, Tony."

His curled forefinger nudged her chin upwards. Their eyes locked, his a determined steel whilst hers filled with unexpected tears.

"Hey, what's all this? I'll be back, as Arnie used to say. Before you wake up, probably." After a quick kiss, he was gone into the darkness, and she had a sinking feeling that he was gone from her life, too.

Some of the partygoers danced and spun her around, and she smiled and jigged a little in time to the music playing from someone's iPod. She then strolled about for the next twenty minutes, her thoughts remaining firmly on the three agents' mission.

Not in any rush to step back through the door that would be filled with Tony's scent, she took the stairs up to the room. As she turned the key and reached for the light, a hand covered her mouth before she could scream.

"You..." she mumbled behind the hand. Fear gripped her insides, making her legs wobble.

The bathroom door sprung open to reveal a second intruder, and the colour drained from her face. *Baldwin!*

Ice filled her veins...then everything went black.

Chapter Forty-Two

With relative ease, Tony and his gang approached the hull of Baldwin's yacht, but years of experience told him something was wrong. *No lights on the boat. No movement.* He leaned towards Weir and whispered, "Something's up."

In the dark, with their eyes now fully adjusted, Weir and Taylor both shook their heads. "It's the middle of the night, man," Weir said.

"I don't give a flying fuck. It ain't right."

"What do you want to do then? Proceed or turn back?" Taylor scanned around them.

The three men gripped the side of the rowboat as it bobbed on the waves rebounding off the hull of the huge yacht. "Let me think for a minute." Tony swept a hand through his short hair, before quickly returning to grip the side of the boat as Taylor moved towards him, almost tipping the small boat. "Sit still," Tony hissed through clenched teeth.

"I was just gonna say trust your instincts, Tony. You know this guy better than we do. What do you reckon?"

He stared at Taylor as though he'd asked for the combination to the safe at Threadneedle Street.

Tony grabbed one of the oars and motioned with his head for Taylor to pick up the other one. They headed back to shore, with Tony deep in thought. *Something's definitely wrong!*

* * *

A kick to the stomach made Lorne groan and curl up in to the foetal position. She gagged on the bile threatening to spill from her mouth.

"Get up, bitch!"

Slowly Lorne raised her head to look up at Baldwin towering above her. His right leg swung back, ready to kick out at her again, and she quickly shuffled back against the door. "No, please. I'm trying."

"You're stretching my patience, Simpkins. Get to your feet. *Now*!"

With her stomach muscles constricting painfully, she inched her way up the door to stand semi-erect. The other man in the room averted his gaze from hers, looking uncomfortable, and turned his attention to Baldwin. Lorne noted how wary the other man looked in the Englishman's presence.

Baldwin let out a crazed laugh and turned to speak to the man alongside him. "Ah, *capitaine*, from the look she just gave you, I think Lorne expects you to help her out of her precarious situation."

The man she'd recently spent the night with shuffled awkwardly and shrugged.

As Lorne watched the exchange between the two men, her mind raced, searching for a way to get her out of her latest mess. As the pain in her stomach seeped away, she straightened to her full height and pulled determined shoulders back against the door. "Huh. The last thing I would want is any help from *him*," she spat, hoping her angry bluff would eventually work in her favour. If Baldwin got the impression that she didn't trust the *capitaine*, maybe he would drop his guard.

The Frenchman's features filled with hurt, causing Baldwin to let out a belly laugh. "I see you left a lasting impression on the ex-Inspector, Michel." Neither of them spoke as Baldwin's amused eyes flicked between Lorne and the *capitaine*.

She carried on with her outburst. "You're foolish if you think you can get away with whatever you're intending, Baldwin. Tony will be back soon." Her eyes narrowed, while his danced with amusement, then annoyance.

"Treat me like an idiot at your peril, Simpkins." He stepped forward.

Despite her insides filling with sudden fear, Lorne refused to buckle under his vicious stare.

"Have you not learnt anything from your dealings with me?"

I will not let him see how scared I am. Tony, where are you when I need you most?

With Baldwin a mere six inches from her and their gazes locked, she found it impossible to see what his hands were up to, but she felt it. As one of his hands roughly tugged at the buttons on her blouse, she heard the loud click of a knife unfolding. *Oh, God. He's going to kill me...*

Her eyes squeezed shut as she anticipated what was about to happen, but then far off in the distance, she heard Michel's quivering voice plead, "Don't, Robert. She does not deserve this."

Baldwin grunted a response and continued his invasion of her trembling body. He tore the cotton blouse away to expose the black lace bra straining over her breasts. Lorne's eyes shot open. Her hands automatically rose to try to cover her exposed flesh, but the sudden feel of cold metal digging in her ribs made her rethink that action, and she dropped her hands again.

She sucked in a breath and held it as Baldwin's head dipped, and she felt him lick and suck at her breast above the flimsy lace.

Wide-eyed, Lorne looked over at the Frenchman for help, but in return he gave another helpless shrug. Refusing to give up, she mouthed "Help me," and she could tell by the way he shuffled his feet that his resistance was faltering, if only slightly.

Pricking up her ears, she thought she heard something in the hotel corridor. Turning her head, she placed her left ear against the door, but her hope died when all she heard was Baldwin groaning with pleasure as he suckled like a newborn baby. With her mind playing cruel games, Lorne tried once again to silently plead with Michel.

Michel slowly bent down and removed something from his sock. It was difficult to see what it was, but she hoped—no, prayed—that it would be some kind of weapon.

Baldwin grabbed Lorne by the wrist, and in one quick fluid movement, he had swapped places with her, pressing his back firmly against the door. One hand held her tight around the waist, while the other—holding the knife—pulled tight across her chest. The point of the blade pressed into her cheek.

"*Drop it*. Drop it, or I'll kill her now."

They heard a thud, and Lorne looked at the floor to see that Michel had dropped a gun. Her heart sank, along with any lingering hope of her being rescued. Michel's face showed signs of regret.

Baldwin's arm tightened across her chest. She felt as if a python was squeezing the life out of her, and she coughed as she fought for breath.

"Rip the cord off the lamp, and bring it to me," Baldwin ordered.

Michel's frown deepened, and Baldwin lost patience. The hand around Lorne's midriff went to grip her chin, forcing her head to remain still. She winced as the blade tore through her cheek, and her knees almost buckled. She bit down on her tongue, determined not to cry out as the pain intensified.

Michel grimaced as the blood dripped down Lorne's face. He succeeded in pulling the wire from the cheap lamp and again attempted to make Baldwin see reason. "Come on, Robert, there is no need for that—"

Baldwin cut him off. "When I want your fucking opinion, *frog*, I'll ask for it. Hurry, give it to me."

Michel held the wire out to Baldwin as the Frenchman's eyes locked onto Lorne's. *Please, Michel. If our night together meant anything to you, please help me…*

Baldwin released the grip on her chin as he reached for the wire, but the blade remained at her cheek.

Michel mumbled something in French. Baldwin snatched the wire and glared at him. Michel clenched the end of the wire and yanked it. As if reading his mind, Lorne elbowed Baldwin in the ribs and managed to escape his grasp. Michel lunged at Baldwin and a scuffle broke out. Lorne searched all around her for something to lash out with but failed to find anything.

Baldwin slashed the Frenchman's wrist. Michel cried out in pain and fell to the floor. Laughing, Baldwin headed her way. *He'll kill me for sure this time…* Lorne spotted the gun lying a few feet away, poking out under the bed. Cursing herself for not seeing it sooner, she dived for it.

"Don't even think about it bitch," Baldwin snarled.

But Lorne's determination outweighed her fear she grabbed the gun and pointed it at Baldwin's chest, stopping the criminal in his tracks.

"You haven't got the guts to shoot me," he snarled.

"Haven't I? After all you've done to me and my family over the years, you doubt my ability to pull the trigger?" She stood up. "Drop the knife, shithead."

Several minutes seemed to slip by before he finally dropped his weapon.

"Michel, get the wire and tie his hands together."

The *capitaine*'s hand was already covered in blood. He stood up and tottered towards the wire by the door.

Worried, Lorne asked, "Michel, are you all right?"

The Frenchman responded by collapsing on the floor behind Baldwin. The criminal laughed, which incensed her. Glaring—and with the gun still aimed at his chest—Lorne stepped forwards and kneed Baldwin in the groin, enjoying the control she had over him for a change.

Baldwin buckled but spat at her feet. "You fucking bitch! I'll make sure you pay for that."

Lorne laughed, "You appear to have forgotten who's holding the gun, you sick bastard."

"Yeah, the bitch I've had pleasure hounding all these years. The copper that always came up short, who I took pleasure in taunting and whose family I ripped to shreds with these powerful hands." His hands rose up in front of him and hatred shone in his eyes.

Lorne's anger made her blood accelerate and her heart thump wildly. "Why?"

"What?" Baldwin frowned.

"Why Jacques? Why him?"

"What, you mean you wish it had been your old man, instead?"

"No. Just answer me." *I deserve to know.*

Still on his knees, Baldwin glared up at her. "Okay, if you want the truth, here it is: Because he had what I *wanted.*"

"*What*?!"

"You heard me. He had *you.* Come on, Lorne. Put the gun down. We'll get out of here and go back to the chateau and watch the money flow into my account. Or if you'd rather, we'll take the yacht and disappear for a—"

"You really are the sickest shit to have ever walked this planet, aren't you?" she screamed at him.

Just then the door burst in. Startled, Lorne's hand jerked, and her finger instinctively pulled the trigger.

The gunshot echoed round the room.

"*You bitch!*" Baldwin whispered as he fell face first to the floor.

Tony crossed the room, removed the gun from her tight grasp, and steered her towards the bed. "Lorne, it's over."

But disbelief forced her to gaze at Baldwin's body as if she expected him to jump up and come after her again. Blood seeped from the warm corpse and began staining the carpet red.

Can the Unicorn really be dead?

Epilogue

"Well?" Lorne jokingly elbowed Tony in the ribs.

He smiled at her and flung a lazy arm across her shoulders. "Be careful, lady. These hands have killed."

Any other day, the smile tugging at her lips would have slipped at his blasé words, but not that day. No, that day was a day of celebration, rejoicing in the fact that they'd successfully escaped Baldwin in one piece. All of them.

Everyone was in a party mood. They had a right to be. The drink flowed more quickly than a flooding river during a spring thaw, on the gloriously warm end of summer's day. Tom was in charge of the barbecue, one hand turning the sausages while his other arm was tucked around Charlie's waist. Her daughter wore a soppy grin, which had appeared the minute she'd learned of Baldwin's death and hadn't waned since.

Jade and her husband Luigi were handing round the drinks and topping up people's glasses even if they declined. Baby Gino was in his pushchair in the shade under the old apple tree, with Henry flaked out beside him. It was wonderful to see everyone so relaxed. It had been a while since that had happened.

"Tony," Lorne warned, jabbing him harder than she had before. "Tell me?"

"Why don't I tell you later, eh? Let's enjoy the day."

"Is it bad news, then?" Lorne persisted.

"Jesus, woman. Don't you ever give up?"

"Ahhh, Tony. That's something you've yet to learn about my wonderful daughter." Sam Collins snuck up behind them and stood on the other side of Lorne. He tucked his arm around her waist and squeezed tightly. A warm glow washed over her as she appreciated being sandwiched between the two men she cared for most in the world.

Sam had joined up with Tony and Lorne at Nice airport, the three of them had jumped on the next plane out of France, leaving Weir and Taylor to deal with Interpol and the local police.

Tony gazed down at Lorne with love in his eyes and shook his head. "So that's what I've got to look forwards to if I move in with you, is it? Being interrogated over the dinner table every night."

Lorne laughed and scoffed, "If you don't tell me what you know, you'll be living on takeaways for months, mate."

"Huh. Nothing new there, then..." He winked at Sam over Lorne's head.

"Tony!" she shrieked, her patience at breaking point.

Everyone at the party turned to look at them, but it was Tom who shouted a warning to Tony. "Hey, Tony... Now you can see why I agreed to sign the divorce papers so damn quick."

"Hey, ex, don't give him any ideas. I doubt he'll be needing any advice from you about how to handle me." She blew Tom a friendly raspberry, and the gathered friends and relatives roared with laughter.

"Come on, you. Let's go inside for a minute. Excuse us, ladies and gents, will you?"

Lorne pecked her father on the cheek and headed through the back door and into the lounge, with Tony close behind her. "Why all the secrecy?"

"It's still a matter of state secrets, Lorne. I, for one, wouldn't want to get on the wrong side of Interpol. Take a seat."

They sat side by side on the leather couch as Tony filled her in on what Taylor had relayed to him with regard to the situation back in France. He and Weir had touched down in London a few hours before and had just finished writing up their reports at Headquarters.

"So, Baldwin was blackmailing Michel, is that what you're saying?"

"Looks that way. He heard about a few indiscretions that occurred in the *capitaine*'s past..."

"Such as?"

"He liked the ladies." As if just realizing what he'd just said, Tony cleared his throat. "But you already knew that, didn't you?"

She blushed, and her eyes dropped to the floor.

Tony picked up her hand and gently kissed the back of it. "I was joking."

They shared a quick kiss, and she urged him to continue.

"He used to frequent the odd brothel or two—not uncommon for French men, apparently. Well, so the story goes, Michel turned up drunk one night at one of Baldwin's houses of ill-repute, and something happened to the girl he bought the services of."

"Define 'something happened'?"

"She died, end of."

"I get it, she died mysteriously, probably while Michel was asleep, and Baldwin seized the opportunity to get one over on Michel."

"You've guessed it. From that day forward, Baldwin had him tucked up nicely in his pocket."

"So, do they know what Renée's role was in the scam?"

"They're not entirely sure, but it looks like Michel and Renée had been lovers for a while. Again Baldwin found out and used the fact to his advantage. With them in charge of the Interpol investigation, it was pretty easy to steer the case in a different direction, even easier to get all the paintings sourced and ultimately stolen. I told you about the Interpol stolen art list, didn't I? Well, Interpol has access to who owns the most valuable paintings, and where they're stored. Simples!" Tony imitated the Meerkat off his favourite TV commercial.

"So what changed? Why did Michel turn on Baldwin, do you think?"

"My take on things is, the last straw for Michel came when Baldwin killed Renée in cold blood and left that note on her body—"

"Note? What note?" That was the first she'd heard about how Renée had died.

Tony sighed and turned away, avoiding eye contact with her.

Lorne repeated quietly, "Tony, what note?"

"I didn't want to tell you."

"It's over now. He's gone. You can tell me now, surely."

"I can, but I don't want to."

"I want you to. We're a partnership now, Tony, and partners are supposed to share both the good and the bad."

"Good God, your father was right. You don't ever give up!"

"You'll learn." She kissed him, and she held his hand while she waited for him to tell her the one thing he was struggling to divulge.

"The note said that you were next."

She gasped. "I'll always be grateful to you, Tony, for dragging me out to France," she said softly, a tiny tear escaping the corner of her eye.

"Is that why you asked me to move in with you?" he teased, wiping the tear away as he held her face between his hands. They shared a deep kiss.

"Get a room, you two," Luigi shouted from the doorway, before he disappeared again. They laughed as they parted, and Tony gave Luigi a delayed finger in response.

She turned solemn once again. "I have regrets about Michel—you know that, don't you?" He nodded, and she continued, "I don't know why I slept with him. Maybe it was his accent; maybe he reminded me of Jacques…"

Tony raised his hand to pause her mid-sentence. "There's no need for you to explain, Lorne. We weren't involved then. It's not like you cheated on me with him. Despite me knowing that I loved you."

She stared, shocked. He smiled.

"You *what*?"

He rose from the sofa and pulled her up on her feet. "Come on. Let's get back to the party. We'll talk later.

"Oh, I forgot to mention: The countries that had their money recovered have agreed that you should be honoured in some way. I told them you wouldn't appreciate that, that you were just pleased to rid the world of Baldwin."

"Wow, that was nice of them, but yes, you're right. I have all I need in more ways than one. What's going to happen to Michel?"

Tony shrugged. "That's up to Interpol. I doubt he'll get away with anything, though, once his stay in hospital is over. He lost a lot of blood, you know."

They rejoined the party just as Tom set fire to the bangers on the barbecue.

"Now, people, you can see why I divorced *him*, can't you?"

Everyone roared with laughter. Charlie threw her glass of Coke on the fire, trying to extinguish the flames. Tom flung his tongs down in disgust and stormed into the house.

Lorne looked at Tony and whispered, "Same old, same old. I think he needs a course in anger management."

* * *

Later, after the party had died down and their visitors had drifted away, Tony and Lorne made love in her bed for the first time.

Exhausted, Lorne rested her head on his chest, which rose and fell from his own exertions.

"Penny for them?" Tony asked, stroking her arm.

Lifting her head, their eyes met and she traced a line down the scar on his cheek that had always fascinated her. "I was just wondering…"

"Oh, what about?"

She chuckled softly. "I was wondering if we'll have matching scars."

He ran a finger gently down the large padded plaster covering her face and replied, "I hope not. I'd hate you to end up as ugly as me." His arms enfolded her and effortlessly pulled her on top of him. "Have you had any thoughts on my proposition yet?"

"Your marriage proposition, you mean?" she asked, puzzled.

"No. Not that. Why, have you changed your mind? Do you not want to marry me, now?"

She kissed him hard, letting him know how ridiculous his question was. Then she let out a long satisfying sigh.

"No. I meant about joining me at MI6?"

"They wouldn't allow it if we got married, would they?"

"Probably not, but at least I'd have sex on tap for a change."

"You'll pay for that, agent boy!"

"Promises, promises, soon-to-be *Mrs. Agent Boy.*"

Lorne drifted off to sleep, content that her family were safe. She could think about the future now and what that might hold, knowing happily that Tony would be at her side.

ABOUT THE AUTHOR

New York Times, USA Today, Amazon Top 20 bestselling author, iBooks top 5 bestselling and #2 bestselling author on Barnes and Noble. I am a British author who moved to France in 2002, and that's when I turned my hobby into a career.
I share my home with two crazy dogs that like nothing better than to drag their masterful leader (that's me) around the village.
When I'm not pounding the keys of my computer keyboard I enjoy DIY, reading, gardening and painting.

Printed in Great Britain
by Amazon